Before the Crash

and other stories
(1998 – 2000)

S.D. Campbell

Kay Cee
Publications

ISBN: 0-9691548-1-X
ISBN-13: 978-0-9691548-1-5

Campbell, S. D., 1974-
[Short stories. Selections]
        Before the crash : and other stories (1998-2000)
/ S.D. Campbell.

Short stories.
Includes bibliographical references.
ISBN 978-0-9691548-1-5 (paperback)

        I. Title.

PS8605.A54862B43 2016   C813'.6   C2015-906779-0

DEDICATION

To my parents, who never stopped believing.

CONTENTS

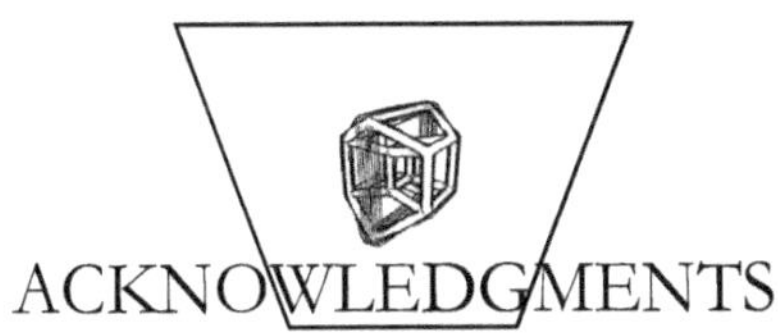

ACKNOWLEDGMENTS

Above all, thanks to my daughter Rhane, for her wonderful ability to share her wide-eyed wonder with her old man. Thanks to all the rest of my family, who have always been there, prodding me to greater success in my writing, but especially to my brother—who tolerates my writer's ego far better than I would.

Thanks to Rigel D. Chiokis of SpaceWays Weekly, Raechel Henderson-Moon of Jackhammer, and Mark Rapacioli of Planet Relish for being the best small-press editors a guy could have started off with. Thanks to Marcie Lynn Tentchoff for suggestions and inspirations, and the occasional poetic instruction and also to Stacie Layne Wilson, who was a wonderful writing partner (now go read *her* work). Thanks to Kent Brewster, of Speculations and the whole gang (at least those I knew when I was there) at the Rumor Mill—I will never forget my first appearance on the Ego Shelf, and was sad to see it go.

Thanks to Aaron MacRae for cheerleading when the early days were hard, and to all of the ASR folks who helped me hone my craft prior to my first publication credit.

I'd also like to thank Phil Klassen and Cathy Proulx who both saw the value in my perusing this project and provided me every opportunity to complete it and make it successful. 10 years has gone by pretty fast.

And finally, a shout-out to Phelan, where ever you may be. We did it boy.

"Faith manages."
- JMS

INTRODUCTION

We have all experienced that moment of change—where nothing will ever be the same again.

It may have happened to you once, or many times, but each time you realize—maybe at the time, or maybe after—that life is now going to be fundamentally different. It is through these moments of change that we grow and evolve as individuals—assuming we survive that singular moment.

Fiction is inevitably about those life-changing events. A fictional story might address the aftermath of the event, or the lead-up to it, or even the instant of change itself. Ultimately however, stories are about change.

Perhaps that is why we can connect so intimately with fictional works—having experienced moments of change ourselves, we can relate to the protagonists and their struggle with the change thrust upon them by the story and the story's author.

For me, the two years between 1998 and 2000 were rife with changes—changes in location, relationships and most relevant to this book, the changes brought about by my headlong dive into short speculative fiction. I was extremely lucky to be able to not only express myself through my fiction, but to find an amazing array of publications to see them in print. The lead-up to the end of the second millennium also saw a multitude of technological, and cultural changes—which influenced many of the short stories I wrote.

This collection presents twenty-three stories of change—all of which published during those 24 months of change and upheaval, both societal and personal. I hope you enjoy them.

Sean Campbell
April, 2016
Calgary, Canada

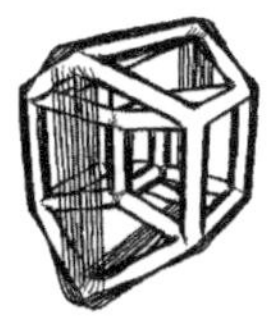

BEFORE THE CRASH

Those headlights would haunt his nightmares for years to come.

The two glowing lamps appeared out of the corner of his vision, and grew more insistent for his attention as they rapidly approached.

Geoff turned to look to his left—to stare into their baleful, unblinking brightness—and time seemed to slow down.

We have only three-thousand and twenty-five nanoseconds.

It was an odd voice that reverberated in his head.

It should be enough for pre-crash processing allocation.

That was a second, unknown voice. Was he going crazy?

The oncoming vehicle has already traveled an additional decimeter. The first voice said, *we are wasting time. Begin access of the subject's parietal lobe.*

"Wait." Geoff tried to say, "Leave me alone!"

It came out as "Laatme met rust!"

Incorrect access. The lateral sulcus has been affected.

Better to bypass language. Time is short.

Agreed.   Two-thousand, five hundred and thirteen nanoseconds.

"Moreugesseumnida." Geoff attempted to say.

Interesting. First Dutch, now Korean. Subject's dossier doesn't indicate knowledge of multiple languages.

"Havercrafte man pore marmahi est?"

Irrelevant. Data is loaded.

The lights were much closer now. Geoff had a death-grip on the steering wheel, but couldn't tear his eyes away from the twin lights that hung only meters away from his face.

Processing. That was Farsi.

He must be going crazy. That was it. In the remaining second before the minivan struck his car, his brain must have snapped—leading to him hearing these voices, and saying these strange things.

Amazing. His processing capability is far more extensive than the majority of other subjects.

Agreed. Look, he seems to be experiencing our activities in real time, and processing them in parallel.

One-thousand, two hundred and five nanoseconds.

Begin the second processing run.

Geoff tried to shake his head—tried to drive the voices out, but he was frozen. Stuck in time and space, he was trapped with the voices as the seconds drained away.

The collision is imminent.

"Usizo!"

Zulu.

Export data. Dump all logs and begin extraction process.

It is a shame to lose this subject's capabilities; he is quite intelligent. The expanded capabilities he could provide...

It is best we leave him. He will remember nothing after the collision and brain injury. It is for the best.

"No!"

Two hundred nano-seconds.

Two voices.

We should not have delayed.

Two lights.

Decoupling IO filaments. Extraction complete.

Too late.

The minivan plowed into Geoff's vehicle at over sixty kilometers per hour. The air was filled with shattered glass and the scream of tortured metal. Geoff felt himself thrown sideways like a rag-doll, and struck his head on the steering wheel.

Suddenly everything went dark.

*

Geoff squinted as he tried to open his eyes. The darkness fled as he found himself staring up into a bright, white light. There was only one this time.

Something was restraining his arms, and he could hear the quite hum of machines, occasionally interrupted by a soft beep.

With great effort, he turned to look to his left, and found his sister's very worried face peering back at him.

"Oh Geoff, you're awake." She said with relief. "You're in the hospital. There was a very serious accident, but you're all right." She gently lay her hands on the cast that encircled his left arm, "Do you remember anything about the crash?"

Images and sensations flashed across his memory. The headlights. The voices. Talking in tongues. It was all crazy and insane. It never happened.

Geoff shook his head.

His sister smiled gently. "I'm sure it will come back in time. How are you feeling?"

Geoff levered himself upright. He was fine in most respects, but it must have been a terrible wait for her. He smiled and opened his mouth to speak.

"Bien gracias. ¿Y tu?"

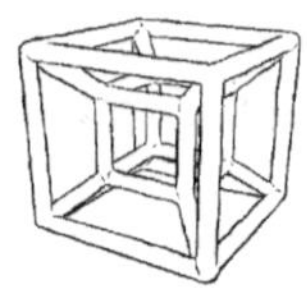

SECOND MOON

I am He who lives, and was dead, and behold I am alive forevermore. Amen. And I have the keys of Hades and of Death.
                                              - Revelation 1:18

*

The people he watched reminded him of those he had known in his youth. They had similar desires, similar dreams, and similar lives. The people were the same, in all their glory and naive wonder.

Only the faces changed.

Michael looked away, knowing that such thoughts only brought memories.

Memories brought tears.

*

The daylight dimmed as the sun sank beneath the flat savannah. The first moon was above the horizon when Toonie returned from his hunt. He had stalked and killed three large rodents known as Ch'thrang. It had been a good hunt, despite his having to range far into the veldt. It had been a day's walk this time. Toonie remembered a time in his youth when Ch'thrang were far more plentiful.

Once inside the circle of firelight the clan's children swarmed Toonie. The noisy youngsters leapt high at the sight of the fresh Ch'thrang; it was a delicacy that they seldom tasted.

But that was for later. Toonie smiled as he handed the Ch'thrang to Mara. She and the younger women would clean them and prepare a feast for the clan. Meanwhile, Toonie was hustled towards the gathering of men. He had been late in coming and had missed the commotion of the late afternoon.

A wanderer had come bearing news.

*

Michael stirred in his rest.

Michael needed little sleep, his body was rejuvenated by short periods of meditation. Tonight—if it truly was night—Michael stirred uneasily. His thoughts rang in his ears with hollow, deathly voices.

Memories long suppressed stirred once again.

"For I am the light and the hope .... "

Michael got up and went to observe his people.

*

The second moon was cresting as they ate around the communal fire. Toonie looked up, watching the second moon spill its bluish glint across the clearing. The two moons' light complemented each other. First moon was scarred after long cycles of wandering the sky, but Second moon gleamed as if new.

Toonie's thoughts were interrupted by the Wanderer's short laugh.

The man was tall and thin, obviously of a western tribe. His voice was as harsh as his weathered face, his laugh just as craggy. Yet there was a glint of humor and intelligence in his eyes that mirrored the second moon's brilliance.

And he told tales.

The Wanderer was a Mennen. Or, so he claimed. His tribe, he said, traced Mennen blood back almost three-hundred generations. Toonie thought about this. There was something about the Wanderer that felt odd. It was said of Mennen that they once wielded great and terrible powers. The ability to fly, to read minds, to tame the very world about them. Toonie shuddered at the thought. Why tame the Mother? She gave, and she took away, but never maliciously.

Yes, the Mennen were said to be strange. None had seen a Mennen since the Elder Days though, and only vague tales were passed down by Bards like Wanderer. Toonie had never met a Bard before, despite being a hunter for nearly twenty cycles. It occurred to him that all Bards might just be Mennen. Who else would want to wander the veldt?

"You look deep in thought."

Toonie's head snapped up with a start. The Wanderer's eyes bore into him. Toonie fumbled with his words, and the Wanderer laughed.

"You should really marry one of those beautiful young women." He said, "She'll quickly straighten your tongue—or cut it off!" The men about the clearing laughed loudly with the Wanderer, while Toonie reddened. He knew that Lissa was at the feast, and he hoped to marry her one day. The time wasn't right yet.

The Wanderer slapped Toonie with a friendly hand, "Why redden, boy?" The weathered one grinned, "I am sorry Toonie, it was not fair to pick on the most quiet." His voice held and elegant charm that Toonie had never heard before, "How may I make it up to you?"

Toonie mumbled.

The Wanderer's grin widened. "Very well, a tale!"

All at the table fell silent as the Bard stood. "Many know me as Wanderer, for no name have I given you. Yet I do carry one, one of long tradition. I am called by my tribe, Mie'kal."

Mie'kal. It was a strange name, one which fell lyrically off the Wanderer's tongue, and hung onto Toonie's thoughts. A strange name from another time and place.

*

Michael's days were filled with work, more than he would have wished for. The price of leadership was a myriad of tedious tasks.

Sometimes Michael would look out at the stars, and wish he could give it all up.

"O righteous Father! The world does not know You, but I have known You; and these have known that you sent me."

The ancient voice haunted him.

*

The Wanderer's voice haunted Toonie's dreams.

The tale the Bard had woven was one of great sadness from the Elder Days, the time before all memory. The Bard told of the coming of the Star, and how all tribes had finally been reunited after ageless wars. There had been hope, and great courage. Only through the vision of one man, The Savior, had the world survived. He stopped the star and saved all peoples, all tribes.

Toonie had dismissed the story as a myth. Who could believe that there were as many people as Wanderer had said? More people than one could count in a lifetime? It was foolish. Toonie's tribe numbered thirty-six, and there were no more than a six of tribes within twelve day's walk. Beyond that was the sand of the desert or the wilderness of the veldt. None lived there.

Yet the Bards told of great lakes that took days to cross, and of giant hills taller than the sky, where, if you climbed them, you could almost touch the Mother. The tales sounded so real.

And where did the Bards come from? Toonie had heard of many Bards tales, yet none of the tribes were home to any. Bards wandered in from the sands, or the veldt. Where did they come from, and why did they wander?

Disturbed by these strange thoughts, Toonie lay on his pallet and looked up at the stars, his thoughts quickly disappearing under the haze of sleep. And in that darkened place, he saw a vision.

*

He was standing in the middle of a strange sheet of rock. It was huge, and perfectly square, its flat, black surface warm beneath him. It was high-night, yet the sky was red like the dawn. Stranger still, the stars were being swallowed by a giant light.

And there was only one moon!

All about him strange people raced. Their cries were chatter, and their pink skin was exposed only at the face and hands, so covered were they by cloth. Nearby he saw fire ravaging a square stone — NO! — it was a hut, but so large that it eclipsed the sky! Toonie was surrounded by them; it was as if his clan's village had been multiplied by a million. Toonie felt like an insect by comparison.

All about him the chaos swarmed; people running and screaming as if they were fleeing a fire on the veldt. Amidst the confusion Toonie was pushed against one form that would not move. He looked up into cold blue eyes. The eyes of a person who knew what had happened.

He was one of the pink-people in the cloth.

And Mother, he had no tail!

"For the first time in many cycles one has found me." The person said in Toonie's language, startling the hunter. *"Your mind is quiet, and you have sought me out."* At Toonie's wide-eyed shock the tail-less man grabbed Toonie and pointed up to the sky.

"Look!"

Toonie watched the red fireball touched the horizon. There was a flash, and Toonie could hear the screams of the blinded for a fraction of a second. Then the shock wave hit, blasting all into oblivion.

Toonie wept at the death of the pink-people.

A second moon rose above the horizon.

*

Dawn was only hours away when Toonie saw the Wanderer leave camp. Without thinking the hunter caught up with the Bard and stopped him. The Wanderer turned cold blue eyes on him, his question demanding an answer.

"What did you see?"

Toonie described the vision, while the Bard nodded.

"I thought you would be one. One who's eyes are open, and could hear his message." He placed an arm around

Toonie, "The great cataclysm that changed our world and birthed our people destroyed his. Now he awaits the time in which he may walk among us, his children, again. He waits for all of us on his second moon."

Toonie was confused, but nodded anyway. The Wanderer walked into the veldt and after a moment's hesitation, Toonie followed. He didn't need to understand now. He knew there would be more lessons.

As the sun rose, the second moon disappeared below the veldt.

*

Michael was at peace.

Below him he sensed the awakening of the world anew. He had waited for countless millennia since the comet had struck the Earth, waiting, and nurturing the remaining life, guiding them towards civilization. In a moment of weakness he had even spread his seed amongst them, hoping to rebirth humanity.

He knew now that he was, and would forever be, the last Human.

It was the younger races turn on stage. For now Michael would guard them from his artificial moon, his machines keeping him alive, and manipulating the environment below to allow for favorable growth. Soon though, when the time was right, he would pass, leaving behind a single legacy for his 'children.'

The second moon.

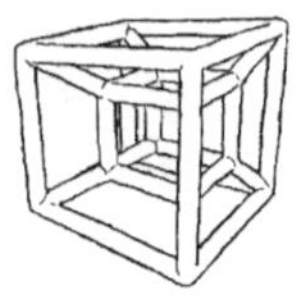

FATAL ERROR

The skeleton towered over him as he walked by, its steel members reaching for the slate grey sky. For the last several months Hal had passed by this construction site on his walk from the parking garage. Most days he never gave the partially completed sky-scraper a second glance. Today though, he paused.

Soon enough these red girders would be covered in concrete and glass, and this skeleton would become full of people making their mindless way through its bowels. It would be a living, breathing office building, complete with drones.

When finished, it would be like every other building in the city; tall, impersonal, and grey. The entire city was grey. The sidewalks were grey. The buildings were of polished grey granite. Their mirrored windows reflected the grey overcast sky.

Hal realized just how depressing the whole city was. He looked about the rush-hour street, looking for a friendly face; knowing he'd be surprised as hell if he found one. He didn't of course. No one cared about a single man, slightly over-weight, staring up at a skeletal building.

*

The morning passed as it always did, in a blur of meaningless trivia. Unimportant matters at the office seemed to eat all of Hal's time. That was why his wife had left him, and taken their children. She had moved to a larger city, where she would continue her meaningless life and raise their children to be drones. Hal stared lifelessly at the report sitting on his desk. Society didn't want individuals, society wanted clones. Efficient clones who would do their jobs efficiently, go home and make love efficiently enough to reproduce, and return to their jobs.

Like some self-replicating machine programmed to do whatever its designers deemed necessary. Like a Von Neumann machine.

Hal looked out the window and watched the construction workers busily putting together whatever they were working on that day. He idly wondered just what the point was. After all, the building would eventually go out of style, be sold, or torn down. It might be burned down by some over-zealous kid with a match. Some maladjusted kid with a match could light a can of gasoline and torch the magnificent new building.

Some mis-programmed Von Neumann machine.

*

The drive home took hours. Traffic was slowed to a crawl whenever there was an accident downtown. A delivery truck had crashed into a car. So Hal waited as the police and emergency response personnel cleaned up the shattered remains of a life and carted it off to the hospital. Hal shook his head. One life, changed forever by a stupid decision. How many people were maimed or killed by stupidity each day? Thousands? Hundreds of thousands?

Hal listened without interest as a nearby billboard blared its advertisement at him.

"Buy Clean-X! Gets clothes twice as clean, with only half the effort. Save more, buy Clean-X! Only $19.99 a box!"

He laughed. How many people even bothered to listen to

advertisements anymore? Everyone was so inundated with advertisements that no one really paid any attention to them. They were everywhere, and what was the point of them if they didn't really sell anything? Then again, what would happen if you removed the advertisements from society?

A lot of drones would be out of work, that's what.

Hal's introspection was shattered as a man in ragged clothes banged his fist on his window. He tried not to look at the man, but he could hear the man screaming something at him. The man pounded again, and Hal rolled down the window a crack.

"We're all trapped in the machine, man!" the man screamed at Hal, "We're all just little cogs in some grand computer. We build and fix the computer, and the user doesn't think twice about us."

The man's stench was overpowering, and there was a mad look in the man's eyes that disturbed Hal. He shuddered and rolled up the window. The traffic began moving again, and Hal pulled away from the still screaming man.

"There's no God, man! Only the machine!"

*

Hal awoke alone in his living room. Outside it was dark. Inside it was dim, with the only illumination coming from the static on the television set. In the flickering light he could see his dog curled up on the carpet. Hal blinked several times and looked around for the clock, wondering just how long he'd been asleep on the couch. The VCR flickered a baleful 19:99 at him, reminding Hal that he had to reset the clock on the infernal machine someday. Ignoring the blinking VCR, Hal stood and shuffled into the kitchen. the dog looked up, but made no move to follow.

The fluorescent light flickered several times before bathing the kitchen in white light. He squinted as darkness was banished.

"There's no God, man! Only the machine!"

Hal shook his head. That street crazy had gotten inside him more than he wanted to admit. It was disturbing somehow. Hal toyed with the idea that the bum was right. Wasn't it always the bums who became prophets? Not that it mattered, if the crazy fellow was right, then there wasn't a God. The bum's 'divine' visions would be coming from who? The machine?

Hal chuckled. God was a VCR.

*

He passed the skeleton again. Today there was more to it. they were slowly closing it in, and soon enough, Hal thought, the drones would be inside. He shrugged and continued on.

As he walked to his office he thought again about the bum who had accosted him yesterday. Hal had hoped that he wouldn't see the fellow again, especially on the walk from the garage to the office. The bum however wasn't the only concern that Hal had. Last night, Hal had dreamt that he was sitting in front of a computer screen; only he wasn't inputting commands. The commands were being input into him.

>LOGIN? User
>PASSWORD? *****
Hello user. This is Unit HAL-1965-M.
>EDIT HALPARM.COM
Welcome to the HAL Parameters Command file.
>INSERT ITEM: renfrew.act

*

"Hal? Are you all right?"

Hal started as he realized he'd been day dreaming. He coughed and nodded. The CEO gave him a strange look, and then continued.

"As you're one of my best people, I've decided we need your expertise on a new account we've picked up. You have to deal with these people very carefully though Hal, Renfrew's is a well-established company, and their people are very specific about what they want. This is a long term contract Hal, through to 1999, and it's very important to us."

The rest of the CEO's words went unheard as snippets of his odd dream floated back to Hal. There couldn't possibly be a connection. His mind was just playing tricks on him. That's all it was, just mind tricks.

Hal stood.

"Maybe you should ask someone else sir."

*

It was at lunch, in the shadow of the skeleton, that the bum visited Hal again. Hal saw him coming across the street, and wanted to duck away before the other man caught up, but the only place to go was the construction site.

The bum smiled with broken teeth. The stench of the man was almost visible as he took Hal by the arm and steered him out of the crowd.

"You know don't ya?" the man with the broken teeth asked. Hal shrugged, "I don't know what you mean." The bum laughed. It was a wheezing, hacking sound that rattled.

"I can see it in your eyes. You saw the machine. You felt the user." He smiled and Hal winced.

"Look, I don't know what you're talking about." Hal said pulling away, "You're loony."

The bum narrowed his eyes, "Let me ask you this, friend. Why do you work where you do? Huh? Why do these buildings keep being put up? Why? What's our reason for being here?"

The bum moved closer, and Hal could smell garlic on his breath. "I'll tell you why friend. We're all just software and hardware in some massive computer. Cogs in the machine. We're here to calculate some problem for the user."

"No."

The bum nodded, "Why not? What's wrong with that? At least then we know we're here for a reason."

Hal shook his head. "I'm not a cog in some user's machine."

The bum laughed again as Hal strode away.

"Look at yourself friend. You already are."

*

```
Hello user.  This is Unit HAL-1965-F.
>EDIT GLFILE.COB
404.  File not Found
>DIR \HAL\GLFILE.*
```

```
404.  File not Found
>DIR \HAL\*.*
FAMILY.COB  HAL.EXE WORK.COB
>GET \USER\MASTER\GLFILE.COB
File Received
>EDIT GLFILE.COB
File Open.
>INPUT var date.conversion=3
Accepted.
>CALCULATE current.date + date.conversion
Error.  Division by Zero.
>RESET
```

*

Hal woke in a sweat, his starched bed sheets wrapped about his legs. The dog looked up lazily from its spot on the floor, licked itself, and went back to sleep. Hal closed his eyes and swallowed. He felt his heart pounding in his ears. In the darkness a dim light blinked a crimson warning

His alarm clock flashed 12:00. The power must have cut out. Hal reached to reset it.

He paused, holding the clock in his hands.

RESET.

He shook his head and set the clock to six in the morning. When he tried to get back to sleep however, he found he couldn't. He ended up tossing and turning, a vague unease making his flesh creep. He soon realized he was afraid to sleep. He was afraid of the nightmare that awaited him there. He was afraid of what he might find.

>CALCULATE current.date + date.conversion

Error. Division by Zero.

Hal snapped out of bed, startling the dog. He rushed to his small desk, where he kept his calendar. The last year printed there was 1999. Hal quickly rifled through his papers hoping that he could find some indication of the strange year he'd seen in his dream. The highest number he could find was 1999. There weren't any years after 1999 anywhere. Hal himself couldn't conceive of a year past 1999.

If that's all there was, what then was 2000? Logically, it should follow 1999 in a decimal based system, but it didn't exist. Hal tried to think of the year 2000, but it was like a fog floating just outside of his sight.

He grabbed his watch and tried to set it to 1/1/00.

DIVISION BY ZERO.

The watch couldn't do it. The year which should exist beyond 1999 didn't.

Hal gasped, as he realized the consequences.

It was October 13, 1998.

*

It was in the shadow of the skeleton that Hal met the bum for the last time. Hal had left work to look for the toothless man amidst the papers and rubbish of the alley by the construction site.

"Now you understand?" the bum wheezed as Hal woke him. Hal nodded, frantic with his new-found discovery. He dragged the bum to the wooden fence of the construction site and drew a two with three zeros following it.

"What year is that?" Hal demanded.

The bum shrugged, "No year I guess."

"So it doesn't exist?"

"Not so far as I seen."

"But it should!"

The bum shrugged. "Why?"

Hal looked at the man. Hal didn't know why it should exist. All night he'd been driven by this terror at seeing this new year, but didn't know why.

Unless...

"The user tried to show me that number last night, and I didn't understand it. Maybe its important to the user that we understand it."

The bum shrugged. "So."

Hal blew his breath out in frustration, "Don't you see? This year should come after 1999 right?"

"Sure."

"But it doesn't! Our calendar will only go up to 1999. We've got another year until we run out of years!"

The bum shrugged, "Then what?"

Hal didn't know. Maybe no one knew.
It could be the end of everything.

*

Hal stood on top of the skeleton. From where he was he could see all the little people on the ground scurry about their business. They looked tiny; each of them had their own worries and concerns. they walked through the city like drones.

Hal stood on a narrow girder and watched them. It was a long way down to where they were. It was a long way down to where they walked unconcerned. Hal laughed, knowing now that it was all pointless. Even if his dull life had meaning, it was going to be snuffed out when the world ended.

Hal would be terminated by a number. How ironic.

With a shrug, Hal jumped.

*

//PROGRAM GLFILE.EXE HAS CAUSED A PERMANENT FATAL ERROR IN UNIT HAL-1965-M//

The programmer looked up at his companion and sighed. "See, still no good. Every time I run the program it crashes another unit."

Percy rubbed his chin and cursed. "The way things look, this Millennium bug is going to crash the entire mainframe. Is there any way to migrate the data?"

The programmer nodded, "Sure, but it's an old machine, we'll probably lose some data in the conversion to UNIX."

Percy shrugged, "Oh well. Do your best."

The programmer nodded.

"There's no really important data in there anyway."

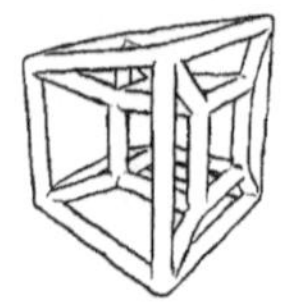

IN A FAMILY WAY

They lay together in the darkness, quietly listening to the sounds of the night. She stirred, and he could feel her looking at him.

"My father is not going to like this." she said quietly.

"I know." he scoffed, "You think I wanted this?"

"Let's get married."

"Are you mad? Do you know what your old man will say?"

"Yes." she answered, "My father will accuse you of being Lucifer's right hand."

He grinned, "We both know I'm not."

"That will not stop him. He can be very short sighted when it comes to your kind."

"My kind?"

"You know what I mean."

The room grew silent once more.

"Well," he said, "Marriage is out of the question. Think of the children we'd have. They'd never be accepted."

"What would be wrong with having children? Just

because other people's prejudices would be offended by our union..."

"Oh please, I think you're taking this a little too far. Look, we've had fun for as long as it's lasted—and let me say I hope it lasts longer—but marriage is a ridiculous fantasy. Yeah, your father's big on prim and proper piety crap. 'No sexual contact before marriage.' Please. This is the twentieth-century, not the dark ages."

"I liked the Dark Ages." she said, bursting into tears.

He rolled his eyes, "I did too." he said, laying a comforting hand on her, "But it's not about the Dark Ages; it's about your father's high and mighty family values."

As the pre-dawn light seeped through the closed curtains, she wept quietly and inconsolably. He sighed. "I have to go soon. Do you really want us to end a night of passion on such a sour note?" No answer. "What the hell's the matter?"

"I'm pregnant."

Stunned, he said nothing.

"I'm carrying your child."

"Jesus Christ!" he jumped out of bed and flung back the shade. Outside, dawn was just peeping over the edges of the clouds. "I gotta get out of here!"

"You said you loved me!" she cried out, "I'm carrying your child; you have to marry me!"

"To hell with that!" A cruel smile touched his lips. "Do what you will with the bastard. Isn't it said that your father loves all children? He should love mine." throwing open the window, he unfurled his bat-wings and prepared to leave. There would be hell to pay if he was late for work.

"See you, toots." he said, flicking his forked tongue.

"What will I do without you?" she cried.

"God only knows." he grinned, and drank in one last sight of her radiant beauty. A single white feather floated up from the bed where she lay sobbing.

"Oh Angel." he said, "You had such pretty wings."

Then he was gone.

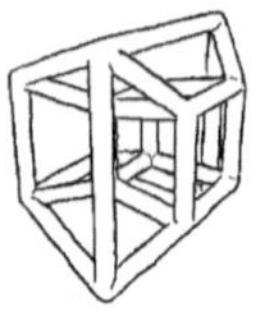

CLIMBING OVER THE FOURTH WALL

Maya straightened and wiped the sweat from her brow. The sun was beating down with a fury that had been unabated since ancient times. She often wondered why the Egyptians bothered to bury their most sacred artifacts in such a blast furnace.

The archeologist set her tools down and climbed out of the pit she'd spent much of the last six months in. The sun was low in the sky, despite the heat, and it made the desert about her shimmer in waves of amber desolation.

From the west, out of the sunset, walked a man.

His tall, well-muscled form wavered in the desert's fury, and he waved as he saw Maya. She smiled. It could only be John.

Suddenly, the egg timer rang.

"Damn it!" Helen swore in frustration, banging her head on her typewriter. It was time to pick the kids up from school. How had two hours passed so quickly? Helen had only finished another thousand words of her novel. How was she expected to finish it at all at this rate?

Grabbing her coat she dashed out the door, wishing there were another fifteen hours in her day.

*

"Doctor Livingston, I presume?"

Maya looked up from her desk, to see a face she'd left ten years in her past. She was used to digging up parts of other people's pasts, but when hers returned to haunt her, it was disturbing.

"John." she said curtly. Her visitor smiled, and entered her office, closing the door behind him.

"You haven't forgotten." he said

Her glare was icy, "I haven't forgotten how you left me alone in Cairo after you proposed to me. You didn't even have the decency to make it to the altar."

John coughed, "You don't understand, I was kidnapped by Palestinian terrorists, and held in Lebanon for the last ten years..."

The phone rang, and John looked at Maya. "Is that for you?" he asked, raising an eyebrow.

Helen sighed, "No, it's for me."

The housewife-cum-writer wearily pushed her chair back, and crossed the darkened kitchen. The phone jangled again, and Helen picked it up, wondering who the hell would be calling after midnight on a weekday.

"Helen Montrose?" A whisper asked.

"Who is this?" she demanded.

"How would you like your fondest wish?"

Helen caught her breath. "What?"

"Meet me in Livingston Park tomorrow afternoon."

Helen stood in the darkened kitchen, holding the phone as the line was disconnected. She gently replaced the receiver in the cradle, but it was too late. Light was spilling from the master bedroom. A pudgy silhouette appeared in the doorway.

"Who the hell was that?" her husband demanded angrily.

"No one." the reply was meek.

The silhouette grunted. "Well, enough of your damned writing Helen, come to bed. You have to get up early and get the kids ready for bed."

"Yes dear." Helen said.   The silhouette waited in the doorway as she packed up her manuscript and typewriter, and quietly padded back to the bedroom. With a satisfied click, the light went off.

*

The park was damp with the late morning rains. Helen shook out her umbrella, and looked about the deserted green space. The sun was trying to poke around the edge of the grey sky, but the cool wind blowing off the river and the morning deluge had kept the park's many patrons home for the day.

Helen sat on one of the benches beside the river and watched it rush past in muddy swirls and waves. Eventually the wan sun appeared, and a light fog began to drift off the water.

From this fog a figure emerged.

He was dressed in a long, dark trench coat that accentuated his gauntness. A black fedora covered his head, and shielded his long face in shadow. He approached Helen and paused, looking down at where she sat.

"Helen Montrose?" the figure whispered.

Helen nodded mutely.

"You have come here for your fondest wish?"

Again Helen nodded.

"You live in a loveless marriage arranged for you by your mother. Your husband doesn't love you, or even recognize your existence unless it somehow disrupts his schedule. Your children are two-dimensional and materialistic, and your life is utterly meaningless."

Shocked, Helen said nothing. The man continued.

"To escape the hell your life has become, you have begun writing a novel. In this novel you have created characters who love each other, and travel the world partaking in exciting and meaningful tasks. You write this novel because you want to be Doctor Maya Livingston."

"Yes." Helen whispered.

"That is your fondest wish." The figure said, "And I shall

grant it, if you so desire. I will allow you to leave behind this meaningless life, and step into the world you have created for yourself.

"Is that what you desire, Helen Montrose?"

Helen thought about it for a moment, and then stood.

"No." she said. "To be honest, I'd prefer another fifteen hours in a day."

*

"Damn it." Maya cursed, banging her head on the keyboard of her computer. In retaliation the machine beeped angrily. Maya sighed. What kind of stupid choice was that? It wasn't true to character at all. Helen Montrose would have chosen to step into her book. After all, that's what Maya's novel was about!

Maya lifted her head, and the computer stopped beeping. Instead the phone began an insistent ringing. With a hang-dog look, Maya stood, knowing she wasn't going to finish her novel today, not at this rate.

"I wish there were fifteen more hours in a day." she muttered as she crossed the living room. The phone rang again as Maya snatched the receiver from the cradle.

"Maya Livingston?" A whisper asked.

"Who is this?" she demanded.

"How would you like your fondest wish?"

MOVEMENTS OF FIRE AND WATER
(with Staci Layne Wilson)

It had been slashed and burned out of the surrounding foliage. The clearing within which the small village stood—his destination—sat squatly amidst the destruction of what had once been lush jungle. In the center of the village sat a small, clapboard church.

Father Michael couldn't help but feel a sense of desecration. Trees that had stood for centuries, rare orchids and nearly extinct fauna had all been destroyed to make way for 'civilization.' Father Michael was proud of the Church's missionary work—the work he did for the church—yet he still felt a chill, as if a darkness had passed across the sun-drenched sky.

Chastising himself for such foolish thoughts, Father Michael picked up his small duffel bag and mounted the steps of the church.

*

If there was a man who could be the complete opposite of Father Michael, and yet remain a Catholic priest, it was Father Josef. Michael was young, well-educated—and though he hated to admit it—rather soft around the middle. Josef on the other hand was rail thin, and so ancient that Michael had a hard time believing the man could possibly have been ordained this millennia. If Josef had walked out of the jungle and proclaimed himself one of the original twelve, Michael would be hard pressed to doubt him. Mind you, there was a hardness about Father Josef that Michael found disturbing. Josef was quiet, with eyelids that always seemed at half mast, yet the hard gleam behind his eyes spoke of countless years spent in the far corners of the earth bringing God's word to the savage locals.

"I don't believe I have ever seen so much rain." Father Michael said not long after he had arrived. He and Father Josef were relaxing in the small rectory at the rear of the church. The rain hadn't let up in three days, and the sheets that fell were so solid Michael was afraid he'd be lost if he stepped out of the church and into the watery blackness.

Josef grunted, "Rainy season."

"Oh." Michael said in awe, "Is it dangerous then?"

"Not at all."

By the next morning two young men had disappeared in the storm. It was said that the Ancient Gods were stealing souls once more.

*

"Ancient Gods?" Michael echoed, his chuckle slightly derisive.

He was lighting candles in the small, makeshift church while one of the local women swept between the pews.

"Oh, yes," said Tshaya, crossing herself. "I am a good Catholic woman," she nodded her head, the whites of her eyes in bright contrast to her mocha skin, "but our God is not the only God."

"Ow!" Michael spat as the match burned out against his fingers. Wringing his left hand, he struck another match with his right and continued lighting the slim, conical candles. There was no electricity in this dismal place, and even though he'd only been here a night and two rainy days, Michael already felt the weight of the darkness on his soul. "Tshaya," he said softly, as though speaking to a child, "There is only one God."

"Of course there is!" The black-robed Father Josef barked as he strode into the room, startling both his young successor and the cleaning woman. "Tshaya, you aren't filling young Michael's head with stories of the Ancient Gods, are you?"

"No, Father," the slight woman muttered, shrinking in the austere presence of the priest she had known since she was born. The priest her own mother had known since she herself was born. Tshaya withdrew from the row of pews and continued her work in a far corner, her back turned to the two men of God.

Father Josef stood at the pulpit and to the empty pews, said a prayer for the two missing boys. "O God, whose property is always to have mercy and to spare, we humbly beseech Thee for the soul of Thy servants, which Thou hast this day commanded to depart out of this world: that Thou deliver it not into the hands of the enemy," his voice was hard as a steel rod, while his body sagged with apparent grief. He made an effort to straighten his ancient backbone and continued, "Nor forget it unto the end; but command it to be received by Thy holy angels, and conducted into paradise, its true country; that, as in Thee it hath hoped and believed, it may not suffer the pains of hell, but may take possession of eternal joy..."

Michael stood off to Father Josef's right elbow, watching and listening in silence. But his mind was practically screaming the question: Why, if those two young men are only missing, would Father Josef be reciting a funeral prayer? Was he only senile (which Michael been warned of before his flight from warm, sunlit Rome to the damp, dark jungle), or did Father Josef know something no one else did?

*

A silent pall seemed to hang over the village now, despite

the renewed appearance of the sun. Michael wondered if this is what it felt like after the deluge. Had Noah and his family felt the oppression of forty days and nights of rain as Michael had of only three?

He glanced sidelong at Father Josef, but the elder priest continued his prayers. Michael waited until Josef was finished and then followed the priest into the rectory. They would take their supper there and Josef would most likely go to bed shortly thereafter. Part way through supper, as Tshaya was serving an aromatic and rather exotic dish, Michael could no longer contain himself.

"It seems rather cramped in here." he said, drawing a scowl from Father Josef, "Perhaps it was the three days of rain, but I feel like taking a walk after supper. Will either of you care to join me?"

Tshaya shrank back, and Father Josef's face darkened, "There are dangerous animals about these parts. They are what most likely took those children. You would do well to stay here."

The discussion was ended.

*

For three more days Michael looked for a way to explore outside the confines of the village, but Father Josef insisted there was too much work to be done, and far too much risk involved. Finally, feeling claustrophobic, Michael slipped away after evening mass and wandered into the dark and steaming jungle.

"No too far." he told himself, "Just enough to stretch the legs." And just enough to stretch his curiosity. A short constitutional, he promised, to clear his head and be away from the cold-fish, Father Josef, for a time.

Not far into the trees Michael stumbled across a discovery. Covered—almost hidden—by lichen and vines sat a squat stone statue. It was obviously of ancient construction, predating the arrival of Europeans to the continent. Michael brushed away some of the cover from the damp granite face to reveal a hideous scowl.

"One of the Ancient Gods." Tshaya said from behind him.

Michael turned, startled, "This?" This rock?

The native woman shook her head, "There was a powerful temple to the Ancient Gods which once stood not far from here. Our village's legends say it burned to the ground many seasons ago. All that remain are these carvings of the Minor Ones."

Michael squatted down to get a better look, "Minor One?"

Tshaya shivered, "Servants of the Great One. The Great One is unseen, and unwelcome."

Michael snorted at such obvious superstition. "Thou shalt not worship false Gods." he quoted, "There is no need to fear stones Tshaya, if you believe in the Father."

Tshaya shook her head, "The Ancient Gods awake, and are taking our souls in the night. They have power even your God cannot stop." Tshaya's face grew as dark as the sky overhead, "Six in the last fortnight." she whispered.

A peel of thunder shattered the sky.

*

Father Josef was saying his rosary when Father Michael walked into the chilly, clapboard church. It was dark, save for the eerie glow of candlelight.

Father Josef, back turned from the door, the gemstone and wood beads wrapped around his hands as he muttered his prayers, cast a distorted, monstrous shadow against the wall. His fingers looked like claws, and the rosary could well have been a writhing serpent.

"Get a grip," Michael chided himself. Tshaya's stories had frightened him, he had to admit. Michael was young, and he'd lived a very sheltered life. Despite the fact that he had left his home in the Midwest at the tender age of sixteen to answer his calling and study the word of God in faraway Rome, he did not consider himself a very bold man. Inquisitive, yes. Bold, no. It had been a mistake to go rooting around outside, finding things he'd rather not find.

But then something caught his eye. Michael's inquisitive side sprang forth again, forcing him to take bold action.

He moved closer to Father Josef, who still had not noticed him. Josef, clad in his customary black robe, continued praying just under his breath. Instinctively, Michael slowed and quieted his footfalls. He squinted, trying to make out the irregular white shape his saw in the old priest's string of rosary beads. Josef was kneeling down and away, and the shadows made it harder still to see.

But see, he did. Michael stopped just short, and stifled a gasp.

No. It could not be. But it was. . . .A tooth. Michael could see the shape quite clearly now. It looked like a human bicuspid, brown with dried blood at the tapered end, nestled like it belonged there between the round garnet and wood beads.

"Impossible," Michael told himself. "It's an animal tooth." As if that made it somehow acceptable.

"And Our Holy Father..." Josef was muttering. Then suddenly, in a strong, booming voice: "You know, Father Michael, it is extremely discourteous to sneak up behind people. Especially elderly priests with heart conditions. Is there something you want of me?" he demanded.

"I - uh, no, Father," Michael stammered. "Forgive my impudence." He bowed his head briefly, then looked up.

Father Josef had put his rosary beads into his pocket and stood in one fluid motion. For an old man, he was surprisingly agile.

Michael had seen evidence of this more than once. And he was strong, too. He'd helped Michael move a bed and a dresser into the tiny sleeping quarters, and the old priest had carried more than his weight despite his gnarled hands and his arthritic back.

"Well, then," Father Josef sighed, "why don't we have dinner then, and retire to bed? Tshaya left us a pot of porridge bubbling on the stove hours ago."

The two priests blew the candles out as the left the

church and headed for the rectory.

*

Five hours later, Father Michael woke suddenly, eyes snapping open to complete darkness. He lay still in his bed, listening.

Aside from the rain, there wasn't a sound. What could have woken him?

He and Father Josef had retired early, and Michael was asleep almost instantly. He'd tried not to think about the tooth during dinner. Instead, he'd asked Father Josef about his calling, and what had drawn him to missionary work. The old priest had been more talkative in that one evening than he had in all the time since Michael had come to live in the jungle, and Michael was so intrigued by Josef's reminisces, he'd all but forgotten about the tooth by bedtime.

He sat up slowly. The bed across the room was empty. Father Josef was gone.

Michael rose and walked into the kitchen area. That, too, was empty. Then he thought he heard a soft chortle. Laughter coming from the church.

He stepped into the drafty room, struck by how the darkened pews resembled tombstones when viewed from the side. He listened, and heard the soft laughter again.

It was coming from the confessional.

Confused and curious, but unwilling to face the icy anger of Father Josef, Michael hung back in the shadows behind the alter and watched.

Some time passed, and Michael eventually dozed off in a standing position. He awoke suddenly when he heard the shuffle of feet. The sky was much lighter outside—dawn was approaching. Silently fuming at having fallen asleep, Michael crept through the silent and empty church to the confessional. It was empty, but a foul odor lingered within. Michael stepped inside and knelt in the position a supplicant would take.

He felt a damp stickiness about his knees.

Startled Michael stumbled back out of the

confessional. A black tar seemed to cling to the edge of his nightgown and stain the knees.

"Vermin." he heard Father Josef say from behind him. "Have a tendency of breaking into the church and soiling the confessional."

Michael turned to find the elder priest scowling at him. Tshaya stood behind Josef, meek with terror. Michael nodded mutely as Father Josef waved his hand in dismissal.

"Tshaya shall clean it before today's mass." he said.

*

The native woman had that evening off, and Michael found her sitting alone in her meager hut. He politely brushed the curtain aside and poked his head inside.

"May I come in?" the priest asked. Tshaya nodded.

He joined her at the small fire that lit the hut's single room. A ragged bed stood in the corner, and what looked like a crude wardrobe loomed over a squat chest. Beside the twin chairs before the fire pit, no other belongings were apparent.

"You live here alone?"

Tshaya nodded, "My husband died several years ago. We had no children. I had little role in the village before Father Josef came. Once he was here, he needed a servant."

Michael nodded thoughtfully, "Then he hasn't been here long."

Tshaya turned from the flickering flames and peered at Michael. "He has always been here." she whispered, a tremor in her voice, "But you cannot always see him."

Chilled, Michael moved closer to the fire. "I don't understand." he said, "What do you mean?"

Tshaya shook her head, "I can say no more." she made the sign of the cross, "God protect me, and you Father Michael. It is not safe to ask such questions. Or answer them."

Silence filled the hut. Finally, Michael asked, "Tell me more about this Great One."

Tshaya shook her head, "I can only say that you are wrong. It was not your God who caused the Great Deluge that covered the world. The Great One and his Minions brought that. They would bring it again, when they have gathered enough souls."

Again her eyes bore into him, deep and enigmatic, "I tell you, you must have faith in what I have said. Speak of this no more, ask of this no more." she turned away.

"You must go. Leave now. There is no more time."

Silently Michael stood and stepped out into the driving rain.

*

The rain was cold against his skin, but Father Michael felt hot. Feverish deep inside. Tshaya's words and her reticence had stirred up all kinds of things: curiosity, fear, questions. He could have sworn that Tshaya had told him, or somehow implied, that her own mother knew Father Josef when she herself was a child. But how could she have, if Father Josef had only come to the jungle a few years ago? "He has always been here..." Who was Father Josef, really?

Michael shook his head, as if to shake the crazy thoughts loose. Ridiculous. And completely against everything he believed in.

First he would pray for strength and serenity, and second, he would contact the seminary and ask them when Father Josef had been sent to do his missionary work here. Everything would be cleared up then, and Michael could concentrate on the job he had been sent to do.

It seemed Tshaya needed some serious ministering. At first she'd called the Lord "our God," and now she was slipping, calling Him "your God." He hadn't noticed any crucifixes in her hut, no statues of the Virgin Mary, no rosary...nothing.

He sighed. It appeared she was still a heathen, even more so than some of the other villagers Father Michael had met. They always had a full church at Mass, but Michael had to admit their attendance was probably borne more out of boredom than an actual belief. What had Father Josef been doing here all these years? Certainly not spreading the word of

God.

Father Michael began to feel angry, and he prayed for guidance under the stormy, dark sky. But his prayers were interrupted and sullied by the echo of Tshaya's words... "He has always been here...The Great Deluge...There is no more time..."

No more time? That certainly sounded ominous. He suppressed a shiver and started walking faster to the church.

Normally, a church was a sanctuary. But this church, with its sad, crooked clapboard frame, looked like a mockery to Father Michael's eye as he approached and entered. It was cold inside, and dark and damp. Michael hated this church.

Shocked and frightened by his own blasphemous thoughts, he crossed himself as he walked between the makeshift pews,

moving quickly toward the rectory. It was cold in there... Father Josef had let the wood-burning stove go out. It appeared Father Josef had gone out as well.

The church and the rectory were cold and empty, but not quiet. Michael stood, listening. Sure enough, he heard it: the laughter.

Only this time, it wasn't coming from the confessional. It was coming from...below.

Michael was sure of it. He knelt down, then bent, putting his ear to the wooden floor. He heard laughter...not happy laughter, but chilling, sadistic chortles and chuckles...and a steady pulsing sound, like drums. Or a massive, all-encompassing heartbeat.

Michael moved around to where the sound was loudest. Then he tapped his booted foot until he found a hollow spot. Bringing a candelabra to light his view, he searched the floor with his hands until he found the slightest hint of a line. The wooden slats had been cut to make a doorway, but the incisions had been cleverly concealed, and Father Michael could see no sign of hinges.

Taking a chance, his heart in his mouth, he banged the door once, hard, with his fist. He sprang back as it popped open, nearly hitting him in the face. His breath held, he waited for...what? Nothing came.

He looked down into the dark hole. He grimaced at the smell. The same smell which he'd discovered in the confessional—a combination of rat feces, sulfur and mildew. The voices and drumbeats were louder now, but still just a din.

There was a convenient rope ladder leading from the rectory, down into the hole. Once again, Father Michael's curiosity pushed his fear to the side. Taking the candelabra with him, Father Michael carefully shimmied down the rope.

The air at the bottom of the shaft was cool and damp, and carried a foul and sickly odor on it. The darkness seemed to embrace the priest, tendrils of blackness seemingly trying to snuff out Michael's poor light source.

From the blackness ahead, the sounds came once more.

Feeling like Jonah, Michael stepped into the darkness and followed the laughter.

The cavern was huge. It looked to have been an ancient limestone cave hollowed out and expanded in the distant past. Carvings of hideous and foul design lines the walls, from which a dim glow ensued. The drumbeats came louder and faster now, and seemed to emanate from the deep shadows of the cavern. Somewhere the drip of water played counterpoint to that primal beat. In the center of the cavern, lit by the wan green glow, sat thirteen figures. As Michael crept closer he could hear their chanting. It was an ancient tongue, and though Michael could not speak it, the words seemed to reverberate in him. Their evil intent was palpable.

Something was about to be born. Something was about to be unleashed. Something unholy and not of this world.

The Great One.

Michael crossed himself Cand began to creep away from this Devil's gathering. He had only made it a few feet however, when his foot slipped and the priest tumbled onto his face into a puddle of black tar. With a small cry he scrambled back, but it was too late. The black conclave had noticed him, and they now turned their attention to the interloper.

As they approached Michael saw to his horror that twelve of them were children. The children taken by the rain. Each of them looked at him impassively with eyes that glowed with the same light as the walls. Tshaya had been right. Their souls had been stolen. Now they lived only to serve their master.

It was the master who terrified Michael. Father Josef reached out a clawed hand and lifter the younger priest to his feet.

"Were you not warned?" Josef hissed.

Mutely Michael nodded. "How could you?" he finally choked into the silence, "How could you turn your face from God and do this to these..." he looked at the children, and words failed him.

"We all serve our Masters." Josef said with glee, "I have only decided to serve one who deserves my faith. God is not the most powerful of Masters. Poor, little Michael, you have yet to learn that. Tonight the Great One awakes, and my centuries of loyalty shall be rewarded."

"Hush." Josef said suddenly, his fetid breath assaulting Michael's senses, "Do you hear the Heart? The Great One awakes."

From deep within the shadows of the cavern the beat grew faster, and there was the sound of shattering stone. "He come, he comes..." the children began chanting.

With his captor distracted, Michael broke free and stumbled away. Josef turned, surprised at the younger man's force of will.

"What will you do?" Josef asked, laughing, "He comes."

Gripping the still lit candelabra, Michael recalled Tshaya's words. Fire had destroyed these demons before, and it shall destroy them again.

"I will see you burn!" Michael cried, "As God is my witness, you will all burn!" Michael waves the flaming candelabra towards Josef, and the other man stepped backwards.

From the shadows came laughter that no human could make. There was the sound of slithering things moving towards him, and Michael began to pray.

"The Lord is my shepherd..."

Closing his eyes, the priest threw the candelabra into the shadows. There was an explosion, and an inhuman cry of pain that would echo in Michael's ears for the rest of his days. From the darkness boiled a fireball. Michael made a dash for the rope ladder.

"Though I walk through the valley of death..."

*

The rain had stopped. There was nothing to quench the flames that engulfed the church. Michael watched for a time, before turning and walking past the silent villagers. he saw Tshaya in the crowd, but she would not meet his gaze.

He could still hear the screams of the children as the fires immolated them. He prayed to God that Father Josef had burned with them.

What had he been a party to? What was that monster?

Would God ever forgive him for what he had done?

Replaying the horrors of that night over and over in his head, Father Michael wandered away from the village, and into the damp darkness of the jungle.

Behind him the night was lit sky as if by a funeral pyre.

*

Somewhere the silence was broken by the slow drip of water. The drumbeats were slower now, and much quieter. The time was not yet right. Yet he had served the Great One for centuries. He could wait a little longer. The deluge would come once more.

"He comes, he comes..."

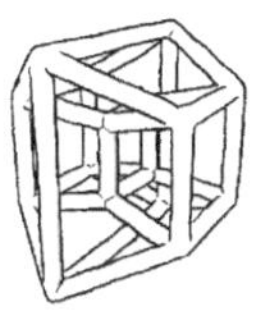

MEIYO NO IZOU
(published as "Honor's Legacy")

The Shinotsuke Valley was dying.

Below her, and stretching to the western mountains, the barren valley lay visible in the wan light.

Shinobu remembered a time in her childhood when the valley was lush with rice fields.

But that had been so long ago.

The Shugenja-Kami's bodyguards lead her across the windswept fortress ramparts. Her journey ended when they opened the door to a small stone room. Sunlight streamed in through the single, narrow window. In the corner a small pitcher of water sat beside a white bowl.

"Wash." the most senior guard said. "He will see you when he is ready."

Shinobu bowed as they left. Stripping her kimono away, she placed it reverently upon the crude sleeping mats. She shivered as the chill air touched her exposed flesh and raised goose bumps. Her usual quarters with the rest of the geisha were deep within the heart of the stronghold, and while the stabled women never saw sunlight, neither did they experience the biting cold of the mountain air.

Many of the geisha had been raised in the stronghold, and had never known a world outside the dungeons they were confined to. Others, like Shinobu, had been stolen from their homes, or sold into the Sorcerer-King's service.

Shugenja-Kami.

Even his name chilled her. It was not, of course, his given name. Once, legend told, he had been born of one of the five families that had ruled the valley. His lust for power had taken him far from the Warrior's Path however, and the geisha whispered that his power came from a pact with a devil. He decreed that he alone could wield the magical forces granted by the valley. All other Shugenja were hunted, and executed. So too the protectors of the valley, the warrior Samurai.

All that remained were the peasants, the geisha and the bodyguard Yojimbo. No others were tolerated, lest they threaten the Sorcerer-King's rule.

Once Shinobu was finished washing in the icy water, she dressed herself once again in her kimono. Then, with little else to do, she sat upon the mats, and waited.

Hours passed. The sun sank beneath the western mountains, and Shinobu found herself cloaked in a darkness as deep and impenetrable as the silence in her cell.

At last the eastern door opened, a flickering light spilling into her room, filling it with obscene shadows.

"Come to me, geisha." said Shugenja-Kami.

Shinobu stood and slipped into the next room.

*

Three nights she spent in the Shugenja-Kami's bed. Three days she spent alone, and silent in her cell. Each day a yojimbo would come with a tray of food, and leave with the empty bowl from the day before. On the third day, Shinobu asked for a sheet of rice paper, a brush and ink. The stone faced guard departed in silence, leaving Shinobu to fear that her request would not be honored. Later in the afternoon however the guard returned with writing supplies. He handed them to her with a yojimbo's customary silence, and turned to leave.

"Domo." she said, as if he was a friend. When she straightened from her bow, the yojimbo was still there, his stony countenance softened. His eyes flickered with lust, an emotion Shinobu recognized with clarity. He reached out a large hand, and gently touched her hair. Suddenly, he paused, and began to tremble. The lust in his eyes was replaced by terror, and the guard turned and fled the tiny stone cell.

Shinobu smiled and closed the door. For anyone but the Sorcerer-King, to touch a geisha was death. Shinobu picked up the paper, brush and ink and moved to the far corner of the room.

There was much work to be done.

*

For five days she was fed by another guard. On the sixth day, the yojimbo returned. Shinobu was expecting him, knowing he would be unable to resist her spell for much longer. Yet she was surprised when he dropped off her rice and left, his face grim and set. For a moment, Shinobu doubted herself and her plan. For sixteen years she had been plotting this, would she now be foiled by fate and a strong-willed man?

She would not.

That evening, after the guards were asleep, but before the Shugenja-Kami's summons, the guard came to her. His chest was heaving as if he had run from the barracks to her cell, but a burning desire was smoldering in his eyes. He quietly bolted the door as she stood.

His grip was like iron as he threw her onto the mats, and she stifled a cry. If the Shugenja-Kami heard them, they would both die instantly.

Then the guard was atop her, their kimono discarded on the floor. The moment was given to passion, and for that moment, Shinobu allowed herself the pleasure of memory.

She was once again a young girl, betrothed to a bushi of her father's house. She had often imagined their wedding night. She could still dream of what might have been.

Later, once the guard had expended himself, they lay together, huddled against the cold. She sensed the triumph within him, and smiled. How little he knew.

"You must go." she whispered, "The Shugenja-Kami will call for me soon. If he finds us together, we shall both die."

The yojimbo grunted and stood, pulling on his kimono. "I will be back." he whispered hoarsely, "When it is safe again."

She nodded, a soft hand gently resting on his thigh, "I ask but one thing." she said, urgently.

He glared at her, "What is it, woman?"

"I ask only for a morsel of fish with my next meal."

He grunted. "We shall see." Then he was gone.

In the darkness Shinobu reached out and touched a sheet of rice paper. The ink was still wet from the haiku she had written hours before. She felt the paper hum with an indefinable energy, and her fingers twitched.

"Soon." she whispered to the darkness, "Soon."

The door opened.

"Come, geisha." the Shugenja-Kami's voice rumbled.

She went.

*

The sun was low in the west when she finally straightened and read the words she had spent the day crafting.

Spine's slow welcome kiss
Glint of autumn sunset
Camellia blossoms

Her hands were shivering even before the west wind blew through the small window, bringing flakes of snow with it. Beside the haiku, on a small sheet of rice paper, lay a small fish head. Shinobu inhaled deeply, feeling the haiku's words fill her trembling body with power. She reached out her hands, her fingers twitching of their own volition. She sensed the valley's power, drawn from the stones and weeds of the fortress. She felt it drawn through the words before her and into her body.

She exhaled, allowing her consciousness to center deep within her. Taking the glowing valley-essence she had gathered within her, she focused on the fish. She picked up the haiku and read the words to the silent room.

Before her the small morsel of fish twisted and writhed. As Shinobu wove her spell, the tiny piece grew into an adult Spine-fish. When it was complete, she exhaled, and collapsed onto the sleeping mats.

There she lay, exhausted, watching the spine-fish's death throes as it thrashed about. After a few minutes its struggles ceased, and it lay inert on the now damp paper.

Shinobu summoned the last of her strength and plucked one of the large spines from the fish's back. She watched as a drop of glittering venom dripped from the tip and spattered on the floor.

Smiling, she plunged the spine into her breast.

*

"Come, geisha."

Shinobu once again stepped from the darkness of her cell, and through the door into the flickering light of the Shugenja-Kami's chambers. Behind her the door closed with a whisper. There was no way back, now that she had started down this road.

On the other side of the room, hidden in shadows, the Shugenja-Kami sat. Between them flames leapt from a brazier, throwing hellish light across the room. The Sorcerer-King stood and beckoned to her.

"Come, tonight we spend elsewhere."

Her eyes flickered to the bed in the corner, but she bowed dutifully. Patience, she told herself, and you will find the proper moment. "Yes my lord." she said.

Shinobu followed as he strode through the darkened corridors of his private wing. She kept her eyes on the floor, lifting them only enough to ensure she was still following him. Eventually he reached a secluded door, and flung it open. A blast of cold air blew across as the western winds flooded in.

He led her outside and into a small courtyard, its sides walled but for the west face, which looked out onto the valley below.

"We sleep here tonight." he said, turning to her.

She bowed, "Hai, Lord."

He swept snow from the central table and threw his cloak upon it. "Disrobe, geisha." he commanded, sitting atop the table. She complied and shrugged out of her kimono. The snow burned where it touched her bare flesh.

"Come to me."

His touch was warm, shocking her with its fire. He made her lie back, his hands caressing her and she felt the icy stone of the table cut into her back and thighs. As before, she closed her eyes and allowed him to do what he would with her body. Her mind roamed free, awaiting the proper moment to strike.

She was still in silent contemplation when he finished. She sensed him dismount her, and she rolled onto her stomach to better see the handful of farms and houses that remained below the fortress. She felt his finger tracing the contour of her back, and she looked away. The wind was now blowing snow into her face, but the flakes stung less than his touch.

"What is this?" His finger had stopped at the small of her back. "Well, geisha?" he demanded, grasping her shoulders and twisting her into an awkward sitting position.

"What, Lord?" She asked quietly.

"The tattoo you wear. I have never seen it before."

"You have always preferred me on my back, Lord."

His slap was like the snap of a bow string. She reached up and touched her cheek, already swelling with the force of his blow. "I ask you again." he said, his voice now dangerous, "What is that tattoo? The Dragon entwined with a sword."

"A house emblem, Lord."

Shugenja-Kami laughed, "No houses exist but mine. That is no heraldry of my domain." he said relaxing his grip on her, "Where did you get it?"

Willing her legs to stop trembling, Shinobu stood and backed away from him. He got off the table as she wrapped her kimono about her. "Answer me, geisha!" he roared suddenly.

Shinobu smiled, "It was given to me by my father when I was thirteen. All in House Nishimura were tattooed with the family mon."

Shugenja-Kami's features contorted, "Nishimura has been dead a millennia!" he yelled, "They died with the rest of the five families."

"Not so." she said quietly, "I am the last Nishimura."

"Impossible. You cannot be—"

"Nine hundred years old?" She laughed. "But I am."

"No." His scream of rage rang off the courtyard's walls and echoed throughout the valley. "I killed the last of you with my own hands." He took a menacing step towards her, but she was already moving away. "Immortality is mine alone!"

She shrugged, suddenly calm, "So be it." From a fold in her kimono she pulled a sheet of rice paper. "I only ask that you listen."

He paused, and laughed. "You have nothing I need hear." he stepped forward, already drawing life energy from the valley for his incantation.

"Wait!" she cried, "Haven't you destroyed enough? You ravaged this valley, and now it grows nothing; its life force dies."

Again Shugenja-Kami laughed, "I care little for that. Let the peasants and their farms die. I don't need them."

He stepped towards her, and his hands shimmered with the force of the valley. The winds whirled about them, the snow now blotting out all vision. Shinobu inhaled, knowing the moment had come. The western wind whipped her hair about her as she unfolded the rice-paper and read aloud the haiku upon it.

Snow upon rice fields
Valley screams in agony
The Dragon's cold breath

A shadow took shape behind Shugenja-Kami and from the blowing snow emerged a draconian form. Its scales shimmered like obsidian in the moon light. Its mouth opened in a scream of vengeance.

His concentration broken, Shugenja-Kami turned to see the monster bearing down upon him. He staggered backwards as the Dragon leapt at him. At the last instant he dodged aside, and grabbed Shinobu.

"If I die, you die with me Nishimura!" he screamed, madness in his eyes. To his left, the dragon turned, and Shugenja-Kami's face grew pale as he looked into the eyes of death.

"For a thousand years, my ancestors have awaited this moment." She said as the dragon stalked them, "As you devoured the five families, Now they shall devour you!"

"You will die!" he screamed.

Shinobu closed her eyes and felt the spine-fish toxin explode from her breast. It burned; a white hot fire flooding through her body.

"Yes." she whispered, collapsing in his arms, "But not by your hand."

She smiled as he dropped her to the cold stone pavement. Unable to feel her body any longer, she closed her eyes and dreamed of warm rice fields.

The last sounds she heard were Shugenja-Kami's screams.

*

In the morning the Shugenja-Kami's body guards found his chosen geisha dead in the private courtyard. She had been poisoned by spine-fish toxin. Her face was peaceful and serene. Of the Shugenja-Kami they found nothing but his torn and blood stained kimono.

In the geisha's cell they found a single haiku.
Honor's Legacy
Tyrant falls and melts the snow
Valley blooms once more

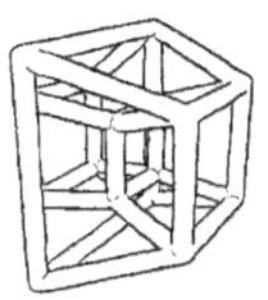

YESTERDAY'S FOOTSTEPS

To walk a league in a man's footsteps, is to know him closer than kin, closer than blood, closer than family.

The Raj'Nunodaa

*

When he was seven, his father brought him before the Oracle. They traveled for days, through twisting, endless caverns, until eventually they emerged onto a dimly lit ledge overlooking a monstrous chasm.

"Tell me of this boy!" his father cried.

There is a greatness within him. The Oracle whispered, *He will be the leader of all men, for a time, but only if he looks into the abyss.*

"Look." his father ordered, pointing into the chasm, "Look within, and tell me what you see!"

Coran saw only darkness.

*

"Coran ir-Almede, Lord of Fareach."

Ignoring the page, Coran strode across the court and kneeled before the Prince. Beside the monarch stood a man in crimson armor. A Templar.

"Sire." he said, "You summoned me?"

The monarch nodded wearily, "I have, my young friend. Tell me, have you reconsidered your position on the Church Tithe?"

Coran looked up sharply at the Templar. "I have not sire. I only voice what the other nobles of the Hearthland feel within their hearts."

"That is?" The prince asked. Suddenly Coran knew fear. He tried to keep calm, but he throat had become dry, and he could not swallow.

"That the tithe is no longer fair. Our tenants slave while the Templars and Church take our harvest. We gain nothing. Alone no single noble can gainsay this banditry, but if the entire Hearthland banded together in this..." his voice trailed off at the Prince's raised hand.

"I understand."

Inwardly Coran raged. Of course the Prince understood, he had supported Coran's motion in council not a month ago. Now, that the Church had sent its might, the doddering old fool wavered.

"You will not yield." It was not a question.

Knowing he was finished, Coran shook his head, "No."

The Prince sighed. "Then I have little choice." he motioned to the Templar, who stepped forward and produced a small sheet of parchment. He thrust it to Coran.

"By proclamation of the Church, as the representatives of the Raj'Nunodaa and God above, you, Coran ir-Almede, are excommunicated from His Church until such time as you seek His forgiveness." The Templar's voice was cold and hard as Coran read the parchment, his hands trembling.

"Ex-communication?" Coran said, "I didn't expect—"

"So harsh a punishment?" the Templar laughed, "You expected to be reprimanded or simply chastised for heresy and treason?" His black eyes smoldered.

Coran looked to his liege, but the Prince only shook his head sadly, "I can do nothing." He said, "As you know, no man ex-communicated from the Church may hold land, title, or position within the Realm." the Prince's mouth became a harsh line, "You have three days to leave the Hearthlands before you're arrested and hung for heresy."

In shock, the parchment still clutched in his hands, Coran staggered from the palace. At his back he could feel the Templar's irrational hatred burning into him.

He was finished.

*

He took only the possessions he could carry. It was three days walk from the palace to the outer reaches of the Hearthlands, and the Townships beyond. Yet Coran feared there was little safety in the Township's farms. The Church's reach was long, and there was a death sentence for heresy in all the holds.

With no money, no food and no hope, he set off.

At the end of the first day, just as the sky was growing dark, he crossed into the fertile central valley of the Hearthlands. The road here was lightly traveled at this time of year, and sprawling country estates meant a soul could travel a league without seeing a house. In darkness he walked several more miles until he saw the lamplight of a small farmhouse ahead.

A dog's barking announced his approach, and as he stepped into the rough cobble courtyard, the front door swung open, and light spilled out.

"Who are yea?" a rough voice asked.

"Please." Coran begged, "I seek a place to rest for the night, and some food. I have been on the road all day, and haven't eaten yet."

The figure in the doorway squinted at Coran. "I know yea." the farmer said, "Yer the one they call Heretic. Ye'll find no room nor lodging here, or from any man this night. Or any other!" The door slammed harshly.

Dejected, Coran continued on into the darkness.

*

He awoke the next morning and crawled from the pile of leaves where he'd taken shelter. His stomach voiced a plaintive plea for food, but he ignored it. He had a long way to travel to make the Townships before the Templars found him, and little time for his body's complaints.

Coran found himself trudging along a familiar road. It was this same road that his father had taken him down in his youth on their journey to the Oracle. He felt the smooth metal hilt of his sword—his father's sword—as it swayed at his hip. With a sense of loss he remembered that magical trek with his father. It was the only good memory he had left of the man.

It was shortly after noon when Coran looked behind him and saw a plume of dust in the distance. As he watched a group of men on horseback charged up the road. They were wielding clubs and other weapons, and we lead by the farmer he had met the night before.

Realizing that they meant to harm him, Coran turned and dashed down the highway, his boots throwing up their own plume. His heart beat in his throat, and the blood was pounding in his skull when he heard the hoof beats close behind him.

Rather than be run down like a dog in the highway, Coran turned and drew his sword. The sparkling blade shimmered in the afternoon heat, as the vengeful horde rode down upon him.

His steel glittered as he slashed at the mounted men. Several cried in pain, and their horses shied away from the flashing silver glint. He had begun to hope that he might hold them off for long enough to escape, when a blow crashed into the back of his neck, and blackness enveloped him.

*

He was a boy again, playing in the yard of his father's estate. It was a hot day, and again, Coran was alone. His father presence had always been a random event in the child's life, and after his mother's death, Coran's only companions were the house staff. Mostly they ignored him, and left him to his own devices. His father was not a well-liked man, by anyone.

This day, however, the staff seemed unusually agitated.

They packed together bundles of food, and spoke in hushed whispers. Coran crept forward to eavesdrop at the window.

"His lordship's taking the heir to the outer reaches."

"To see the Oracle, they say."

"Och. It's a fool's errand. They'll both be killed."

"Good riddance, if you ask me."

A shadow fell over Coran, and he turned and looked up at his father's face. That weathered countenance was as stern as always, yet there was an uncommon light in the man's dark eyes.

"Come." He said gently, "Let us hear God's voice."

*

When Coran opened his eyes, he was nearly blinded by the light. He quickly closed them, and tried to silence the ringing in his ears.

A shadow blocked the light. "So, Lord Fareach has been reduced to this, a pitiful body brought before God." Coran recognized the voice. It was the voice that had finished him.

Rough hands picked him up by the shoulders, and Coran opened his eyes to see the Templar's face looking at him in disgust.

"Pitiful." the man spat, "You should not have challenged the Church. Too much pride to pay our tithe, but not enough wits to escape the penalty." the Templar chuckled. His black eyes were an abyss of death.

"Where are the rest?" Coran croaked. "Witnesses?"

"No need." The Templar said cruelly, "I shall kill you. Alone. Without witnesses."

"Why?"

"You nobles took my family from me." he said, "My father died in debt to nobles. My family were sold as slaves." The Templar's eyes flashed, "For that I will see all of you arrogant fools humbled before God!" Coran saw his own hatred reflected in those eyes, and he knew he was finished.

"Kill if that's your wish." He said, his hand wrapping about the dagger in the Templar's belt. "But don't kill in God's name!"

Coran jabbed the stolen knife into the Templar's side, and twisted. With a cry the other man dropped Coran and fell backwards, bleeding into the grass. Coran crawled over and watched as the light died from those black eyes.

"No." he whispered, "Not in God's name."

*

Coran fled aimlessly for what seemed like days, desperate to escape. It wasn't until he reached the portal in the cliff wall that he realized he'd retraced the path he and his father had traveled so long ago.

He reached out and touched the smooth rock. His father's voice still echoed in his ears, "Here we leave the over world, and enter the Oracle's domain, my son."

"Yes." Coran whispered, "Now I see my path."

Following his father's footsteps, Coran stepped through the portal, and was whisked away into darkness. Through a maze of tunnels he flew, propelled by mystical winds towards his destiny. Towards the ledge where it all began so long ago.

*

"Darkness?" His father screamed, "Useless bastard!" Coran cringed as his father's wrath turned upon him. "You were to see greatness!"

The young Coran cringed as his father struck him, "You were to lead our people from the Church's yoke!" again the blow fell, "You were to be my heir!"

"No father!" Coran wept, "I saw greatness, I saw it!"

His father paused, his hand raised, "What?"

"I saw it, father." Coran said.

"What did you see?" his father rasped.

"I saw God." the boy lied.

*

Once again Coran stood on the precipice and looked into the darkness below. A terrible wind buffeted him, and he grasped the railing to keep from plummeting over.

"I looked into the abyss, Father." He said above the howling winds. He remembered the hatred in the Templar's dark eyes; the same hatred he saw in his father's.

"I saw fear, and hatred and death." he cried, "Is that what you wanted? You wanted me to hate, and to kill?"

You also saw love. The Oracle's voice whispered.

Coran fell to his knees and wept. "Yes. In my father's eyes." he trembled before the sound and fury, "God forgive me, I did see love."

You have no family. It was not a question.

"I have nothing." Coran sobbed as the wind died.

Join my family. the voice whispered, *They need you.*

Coran looked up. Across the ledge stood a lone man in dark robes. Flanking him, in brilliant armor, stood two Templars.

My church needs a leader. the voice said, *My people need a leader. You will lead them. Until the Messiah comes.*

"Me?" Coran's voice trembled, "After my heresy?"

You are loved. the voice whispered, *You are forgiven.*

And Coran understood. All his life had been leading to this. The frightened, lonely child; the proud, arrogant noble; and finally the broken exile had been led here. He had followed yesterday's footsteps expecting only exile but instead had found a family.

He stood and prepared for all his tomorrows.

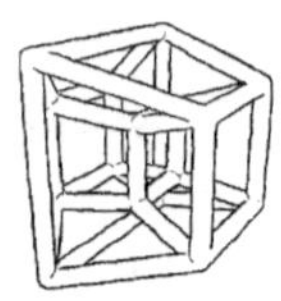

MEMOIRS OF AN INTERGALACTIC DIPLOMAT
(Or How to Eat an Antarean and Get Away with It)

The universe changed on January 1, 2000.

I remember that day well. It was a Saturday, and it snowed in Ottawa. That, of course, was not surprising. It always snows in Ottawa in January . The real difference was that January 1, 2000 was the day the aliens landed.

It was also the day that the world computer net crashed, but that isn't very important.

Of course, as any school child would know, the Antareans landed just outside every major city in the world in the hopes of making peaceful contact with us.

What any school child doesn't know is that on January 1, 2000 at approximately eight in the morning a hunter in the Ozarks almost started an intergalactic war. The problem with the Antareans, you see, is their ears. Actually it's their ears, tail and sundry other distinguishing characteristics that are so similar to a common terrestrial lagomorph that if you put a drum in an Antarean's hand, you'd swear they were auditioning for a battery commercial.

The pink fur should have tipped off Jim Bob. It didn't, and he and his family ended up eating Antarean stew for the next week(I am told it tastes remarkably like chicken).

Suffice to say the Antareans were mildly annoyed. Luckily the Supreme Commander had landed just outside Ottawa, and I was one of the first people to go an meet his delegation. The Prime Minister felt that my post as Minister of External Affairs made me best suited to deal with aliens. My team and I arrive by helicopter to the landing site at about nine in the morning, Ottawa time. There was quite a ruckus in progress, as the CBC had beaten us there by several minutes and were scrambling for interviews. As I approached the Supreme Commander was telling the CBC reporter that his ship had been on approach to Toronto, but had hit a bad spot and overshot its target. After he had killed his navigator, it was decided that his craft would land beside 'That small riverside dung-heap.' The Universal Translator wasn't working at the time of the quote, as clearly indicated by the Supreme Commander's assertion later that "That was taken out of context."

All in all, the Supreme Commander was a thoroughly likable sort, after it was explained that we took some offense to the Antareans exterminating our species. The Supreme commander explained quite politely that that was first contact procedure in instances such as these. In the event that an Antarean was attacked or killed (and Jim Bob had done both to several) standard operating procedures were to exterminate the offending species and make contact with the next available sentient race. I understand the Supreme Commander was quite looking forward to speaking with a Dolphin.

I asked the Supreme Commander if I could have some time to look into this matter. He complied, but did request that we restock his ship with several bushels of brussel sprouts. After placing the requisition, I promised the Supreme Commander that I would contact him as soon as I had sorted out this diplomatic incident. He thanked me, and I immediately headed back to my office to contact my American associates.

The next few hours were rather frantic as I not only had to find out exactly what had happened in the Ozarks, but I also had to dodge an American President who denied any allegations that aliens had landed on American soil. He ended up rather red-faced when our Prime Minister announced that contact had been made just outside Ottawa, and that Canada was in negotiations with the Antareans. Then news broke that the Antareans were contemplating war. I turned on the television at eight that evening to find the Supreme Commander giving an interview on the Larry king Show.

The President vehemently denied that an American citizen had attacked an Antarean. Then the Speaker of the House of Representatives held a press conference stating unequivocally that the American people were guaranteed the right to bear arms, and if an illegal alien had trespassed onto this man's private property and was injured, it was too damned bad.

The Supreme Commander phoned me at three the next morning. He was calling to let me know that, because the murdered first contact team had been led by his mother-in-law, he'd give us three months Antarean Standard Time, to prove to the Antarean delegation that our race was worthy of survival.

I asked how long three standard months were in Earth time. The Universal Translator hummed and hawed.

"Forty-eight hours?" the Supreme Commander said.

It took me several more hours to convince the American Secretary of State that I should be allowed to see Jim Bob. It wasn't until the Antareans began moving large ray-guns planet-side and asked for (and received) a meeting with the Dolphins, that the Americans allowed me to see the man who had started this incident twenty-four hours before.

Jim Bob was being put up in a maximum security facility, guaranteed by the CIA, FBI and US Army to be able to repel any and all Antarean Assassination Squads. I marveled as I entered the building. They had made it look exactly like every other Hilton in the world.

After being directed to room 212 by a Navy SEAL cleverly disguised as a maid, I found Jim Bob amidst a bustling group of armed persons. Each had that shifty-eyed look of a paranoid maniac, so I knew immediately they were American security specialists. Jim Bob was watching Geraldo, where, to my surprise, the Supreme Commander was giving an exclusive interview.

"I understand you've broken off negotiations with the American Government." Geraldo said.   The Supreme Commander shook his head, his ears flopping about.

"Not at all.   We were never negotiating with the Americans. our negotiations with your people are being conducted with The Right Honorable John Alison McKinnon, Member of Parliament for Malpeque."

"Who?"

"He's a Canadian."

The studio audience booed.

"Anyone have a brussel sprout?"

The next several hours passed quickly as I debriefed Jim Bob. I was stunned by how well educated and well-spoken this man was. He was nowhere near the level of stupidity I had attributed to him.

"Well shucks." He said as I returned from the washroom. "Had I known them there rabbits was so valuable, I'd ha never sot 'em."

"Weren't you suspicious when you heard them speak?" asked my secretary. Jim Bob shook his head. My secretary continued, "Didn't you see the fur?"

"Fur?" Jim Bob asked.

"They're pink!"

"Naw." Jim Bob said after thinking for a minute. "Altho' Ah recon I do think it were strange that them there rabbits tasted like chicken."

"You ate them?" my secretary cried.

"Yes ma'am. Them's good eating."

It was at that point that I realized we were doomed.

I went to see the Supreme Commander later that night. The Canadian Government had gone all out and gave his delegation quarters in my office. They had partitions erected to divide the ample floor space into six spacious suites measuring three feet on a side. The Supreme Commander was lounging in his cubicle when I entered. He looked up from where his wife was scratching his ear, and the thumping of his foot ceased.

"Ah, The Right Honorable John Alison McKinnon, Member of Parliament for Malpeque, please come in. Can my mate offer you some sexual stimulation?"

I opted to ignore the Universal translator's error until the Antarean female offered me a brussel sprout. I smiled graciously.

"An er, aphrodisiac." the Supreme Commander said as he gnawed on the vegetable. "How may I help you The Right Honorable John Alison McKinnon, Member of Parliament for Malpeque?"

"Er, quite." I said as I ate the brussel sprout. "You may call me John if you like Sir."

He smiled, "And you may call me Fluffy, John."

"Thank you."

"You look distressed John." the Supreme Commander said. By way of reply I took out one of my few remaining cigars and sighed.

"I'm afraid that I've been quite unable to find anything that might mollify your people. While you have all of Earth's sincerest apologies for the deaths of your people, there's very little we have to offer..."

The Supreme commander paused and sniffed the air. His eyes fell upon my unlit cigar and refused to move from them. "What is that?" he demanded.

I removed the cigar, "It's er, a cigar. We smoke it for pleasure."

"Remarkable. May I see it?"

I placed the cigar in the Supreme Commander's small hand. He ran his nose over it, and an odd look came over his face. his foot began thumping madly, and I feared he'd gone into some sort of seizure. I was about to offer some assistance when he stopped thumping.

And promptly ate the cigar.

"That was exquisite." he said in ecstasy. "I believe John that we have found something that will save your species. This cigar is the most incredible morsel I have ever eaten. If you agree to supply my people with all the cigars we want, at a reasonable price of course, the Antarean people will grant a full pardon to Earth."

I nodded, pale with relief. We shook hands on it, and as I left the Supreme Commander turned to me, a thoughtful look on his face.

"The Dolphins don't grow cigars do they John?"

I shook my head.

"Pity."

*

The rest is, to coin a phrase, history. The world's tobacco companies, for years facing oblivion at the hands of health conscious governments, had a new lease on life. Earth immediately began to ship millions of tons of hand rolled Cubans to Antares each year. The Antareans, ever grateful patrons, even deigned to give us access to their Flummox Drive, the only known way to traverse faster than light. Within the decade Earth was admitted into the United Federation of Orbs, and I was assigned as ambassador-at-large for all of our solar system, even if the Dolphins did protest the vote.

To this day however, not one Antarean has ever attempted another landing on Earth. Suffice to say, the Dolphins are mildly annoyed.

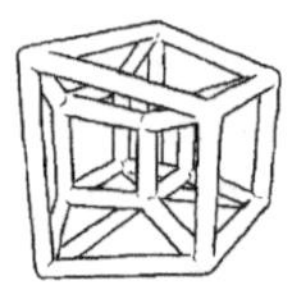

SHINED, SEALED AND DELIVERED

Kylen often thought having a sister who just happened to be a gorgon was a drag. Kylen was willing to admit however, that it was worse when she was your only family. She'd lived with her sister Sepia under the ruins of the family keep for the last eight years. It was a comfortable, if dusty, complex of caves and tunnels, but it lacked one thing that every sixteen year old girl wanted to have.

"Boys." Kylen grumbled as she shined the suit of armor in the entrance cavern. "When your sister's a gorgon, boys just don't come knocking do they, Cantrip?"

The stone bat that sat perched on the suit's shoulder gave a muffled cheep. Kylen sighed and picked up the tiny statue.

Another problem with living with a gorgon. Pets had a tendency to become petrified.

"I told you not to peek in when she was bathing." Kylen

scolded, "You know how she can get after a long day in the library."

The bat meeped sullenly. Kylen shook her head and put down the polish brush. What Kylen really wanted was an excuse—any excuse—to get away from the caves, and to meet some people her own age.

She stepped back and looked at the armor, and gazed at her own reflection. It wasn't much fun, but polishing armor was the only hobby available these days. She looked at the suit with a critical eye.

"You know what, Cantrip?"

The bat chirped an inquiry.

"Dad's old armor is missing something."

Cantrip clicked several times in rapid succession, and Kylen nodded. "Exactly." She patted the suit of armor on the shoulder and cocked her head to listen down the corridor.

A gentle hiss indicated her sister was napping.

"Come on, Cantrip." Kylen said, placing the bat statue on in a small pouch, "If we hurry we can get into town, and buy a few accouterments before Sepia wakes and wants me to shampoo her snakes."

With a bounce in her step, and a full pouch of coins in her hand, Kylen skipped out of the cave and down the path towards the town below.

*

The town of Clear Springs was a bustling little settlement. It was the only major establishment within several leagues, and many of those who farmed the surrounding fields came to Clear Springs to sell their excess produce, and buy much needed supplies and services.

Since the fall of her family's Keep, however, Kylen had noticed that some shops were not faring as well as they had under her father's benevolent rule. The local armor smith, was one such unfortunate. With the loss of the Duke's coin, Old Murder's Armor was facing lean times. Few farmers required armor for working their fields, and after the sack of the Keep, even fewer Knights passed this way.

A small bell tinkled as Kylen entered the armor smith's shop. The smell of fresh leather and hot metal greeted her nose, and a blast of heat blew past her and out the door.

"The forge is full." a voice called from the back room, "We can have those plowshares ready by next..." the voice trailed off as a tall young man entered the from the back. He cleared his throat and bowed to Kylen, "My lady."

Kylen blushed, "Hello."

"My father's in the back, if you're looking." the boy said, flustered, "Unless I can help you."

Kylen nodded, "I'm sure you can be of service." she took out her pouch of coins and placed it heavily on the counter, "I need a few accessories." she said smiling.

"Accessories?" the boy asked in surprise, "What kind of accessories?"

Kylen hesitated, "Um. I need a shield." she said. The boy opened the purse and his eyes went wide. There was no small amount of coinage within.

"My father can have his best readied and delivered to you by tomorrow."

Kylen nodded her thanks, and turned to leave. At the threshold, she turned back to the still wide-eyed lad. "I'm rather new to this town." she said, "Where could I find a quiet place for supper?"

The young man stepped from behind the counter and pointed down the street, "The Flying Buffalo is our local inn. It's just up the street from here." He paused, and his Adam's apple bobbed, "If you don't mind, I could take you there."

Kylen smiled, "I would be honored, kind sir."

The lad offered his arm, "My name is Rufus." he said nervously as Kylen took his elbow.

"Kylen." she said and indicated for him to lead on.

*

Going to dinner with a boy wasn't all that difficult, Kylen decided. At least you could look at him while you were speaking. Supper at home was always difficult, especially when one unwitting glance across the table could turn you into a lawn ornament.

Mind you, Kylen thought, Sepia did talk about interesting stuff. Her magical research, her latest spell or potion were all fascinating supper-time topics.

Rufus liked to talk about armor. Leather armor, chain mail, plate mail, helms, and shields all seemed to fascinate the lad.

Kylen was bored silly.

Still, this was the first time she'd been able to meet with a boy since her eighth birthday party. Despite it all, Kylen enjoyed talking with someone her own age.

"The links are very small and intricate." Rufus was saying, as they finished supper, "And it takes a very steady hand to ensure they mesh together properly. If you have a badly constructed piece, it could gouge the wearer. Very painful"

Kylen nodded automatically, "I see."

Suddenly, a muffled meeping came from the pouch about Kylen's waist. Rufus raised an eyebrow as Kylen, embarrassed, opened the pouch.

"Cantrip, hush." she hissed.

"Um, what is a cantrip?" Rufus asked, confused.

"Nothing, I—oh my lord!" Kylen leapt out of her seat, noticing the darkness outside, "I'm late. My sister will murder me!" Kylen quickly gathered up her stuff as Rufus stood, somewhat shocked. "I'm sorry." Kylen apologized, "I have to get home, before my sister throws a tantrum at my absence."

"Is your sister such a monster?" Rufus asked, as he followed Kylen out of the inn and onto the now quiet street. Kylen laughed, awkwardly.

"You have no idea."

Rufus grinned stupidly, "I have a sister too."

"Hm-umm." Kylen nodded, making sure Cantrip was still safely ensconced in her pouch, "That merchandise will be delivered tomorrow morn?" she asked absently.

"Oh yes!" Rufus said. Suddenly there was an awkward silence. Kylen wasn't quite sure what to say to a boy who had taken her out to dinner.

"Well..." she started.

"Will I ever see you again?" Rufus asked desperately.

"Sure." Kylen said, "If you make the delivery tomorrow." she pointed towards the looming ruins on the hill, "Just drop it off at the cave entrance below the ruins of the main gate."

Rufus beamed. "I'll be there!" he said, and leaned over, quickly stealing a kiss before he ran off down the street. Kylen watched him disappear into the darkness, and rubbed the spot where his lips had caressed her.

A boy had kissed her!

Humming a jaunty tune, Kylen set off home.

*

Breakfast was a sullen affair.

Sepia refused to talk to Kylen except to hiss for the milk pitcher. Kylen's lark had meant that Sepia was forced to shampoo her own snakes, a task she found exceedingly awkward without the use of a mirror. A task she spent much of the night before lamenting to Kylen about.

"Because of your selfishness, I bit myself." Sepia said as Kylen was clearing away the dishes. She showed Kylen her swollen finger, "I had to suck the venom out myself."

Kylen snorted, "If you find shampooing your snakes such a chore, get yourself a mirror!" she said as she carried the dishes into the kitchen cavern.

Sepia huffed and strode towards her study.

Kylen glowered after her. In the corner Cantrip chirped disapprovingly. Kylen turned to the bat statue and glared at it too.

It was late morning when Rufus arrived with the package. It was a large metal affair, and its surface shone like a reflecting pool.

"It's beautiful." Kylen said. "But..."

Rufus poked his head over the top, "My father's best." he grunted, his arms straining, "Bloody heavy too." he said with a grimace.

"Not to worry." Kylen said, leading him into the caverns, "I just want you to place it beside my father's suit of armor."

She glanced at the shield, wondering how she could score its surface. Perhaps acid?

"Your entire family lives here?" Rufus asked incredulously. Kylen shook her head, distracted.

"Just my sister and I. My parents died some years ago." She pointed to the armored suit standing in the corner, "You can put it just over there." Now where was that acid?

"You know, I could take you away from all of this." Rufus said as he struggled across the room, "My father pays me well. We could be married, and..." stumbling over a rough spot on the stone floor, he tumbled forward and crashed into the armor, sending it crashing to the ground.

"Rufus!" Kylen dashed to his side, "Are you all right?"

Rufus winced and sat up, the package still clutched to his chest, "See, not a scratch." he said, with a weak smile, "I hope I didn't damage anything too badly."

"Kylen?" Sepia's voice hissed from the next cavern. Kylen's face grew ashen as she heard the patter of running feet. She couldn't look. Knowing what was coming next, Kylen closed her eyes.

"Kylen, who—" Sepia's voice stopped in mid-sentence. Rufus didn't even have time to voice the words that tried to tumble from his mouth.

After everything had been quiet for a couple of minutes, Kylen opened her eyes and peeked about the room. In the doorway, a gorgon statue stood, frozen in mid stride. Across from it, another statue clutched a polished silver shield to its chest.

Kylen sighed and went to find a chisel.

Living with a gorgon was a drag.

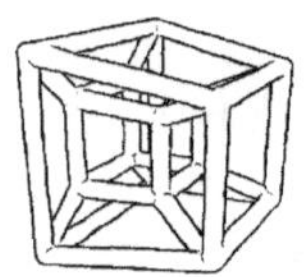

MORE MEMOIRS OF AN INTERGALACTIC DIPLOMAT
(Or Christmas on Eta Cassiopeia)

Eta Cassiopeia is a very black and white system. No, that's not quite correct. Eta Cassiopeia is a very blue and red system. Several hundred years ago the purple skinned Cassiopeians went to great lengths to 'purify' their genetic make-up.

One half of their race, the Red Cassiopeians, migrated to the companion satellite of Eta Cassiopeia IV. The remaining Blue Cassiopeians stayed on the home world.

They have been at war ever since.

I am told that somehow this has something to do with an ancient Earth television show.

*

"This was why we were interested in contacting your people in the first place." The Supreme Commander of the Antarean people said. We were having an enjoyable conversation aboard his vessel some hundreds of light years from earth. Rather, he was enjoyably conversing, and I was looking for a comfortable spot in my luxurious quarters.

"Earth, you see." The Antarean continued, "Has transmitted a wholly disproportionate amount of radio waves in the short time your species has been sentient."

"Disproportionate?" I asked with a wince as I bumped my head against the three foot high ceiling.

"Quite." The Supreme Commander said munching on a Brussels sprout, "After all, it was all your television shows that gave rise to galactic civilization several thousand years ago."

I winced again, this time at the temporal paradox. I am told that traveling faster than light from one point in the universe to any other will also shift you a random number of years through time. How the United Federation of Orbs can handle internal governmental matters when most of its member worlds are separated both by several hundred light years, and several thousand years, is a mystery to me.

It seems to work well enough however.

"Pray continue." I said, stretching my legs to the full four feet I was allowed.

The Antarean scratched his fuzzy pink ear, which promptly flopped to the side and looked at me quizzically, "You have no idea how influential the spread of human ideas has been?"

"Not in the least." I pulled out a cigar and the Supreme Commander eyed it hungrily. I sighed and passed his one. His little pink nose twitched with pleasure, and his hind paw began a rather distracting thumping on the deck plate. My eyes began watering again.

Three years I had traveled with the Antareans and I still found myself allergic to the rabbit fur.

The Supreme Commander nodded sagely, "Well, I see I will simply have to show you. Have you ever been to Eta

Cassiopeia?"

I indicated I hadn't.

"Excellent. I will show you an example of how human philosophy has influenced the development of this species."

"I hope that doesn't take you out of your way." I said with a sniffle.

"Not in the least. We have an arms shipment to drop off to the Cassiopeians anyway, so it'll be no bother at all." He looked at me and munched on his cigar thoughtfully. "Are you all right, old friend?"

I wiped the water from my eyes and smiled.

"Of course, never better."

*

In the three years I'd been traveling with the Antareans as Earth's Ambassador-at-large to the United Federation of Orbs, I had seen many strange and wonderful sentients, but none of them were human. I suppose that was because I'd been back and forth across several thousand years of time in my travels, I was lucky I hadn't met up with myself.

The Supreme Commander—Fluffy to his friends—once tried to describe the temporal physics that was the key to the development of the FTL Praw Drive. It made my ears ring. Needless to say, I was not surprised I met no other members of my kind.

That was not to say I was not susceptible to loneliness. It was especially bad when December 25 of each year came about. Christmas had always been a special day to my family. Three years I spent celebrating it with pink bunny-rabbits.

It isn't quite the same.

December 24 arrived as we entered the Eta Cassiopeia system. I suspected I would have another lonely Christmas on an alien world.

Instead I was pleasantly surprised.

*

"War may be hell, but nothing else is quite so profitable for arms merchants."

I had to agree with the Supreme Commander. He and I

had just disembarked from the Antarean vessel, and I was in the process of stretching my cramped muscles when I heard the distinctive sound of falling shells.

The identification of such sounds can often mean the difference between life and death for a soldier, and thus the sounds of falling artillery shells is often considered by civilians as the most recognized sound to a soldier.

Having been a member of the Canadian Forces myself some time back, I can assure those of you who are reading this that that is not true. The sound most recognized by any soldier is that of a can of beer being opened.

Artillery shells come next however.

Long forgotten instincts took over and I found myself lying in a nearby pool of mud awaiting the end of the world as I knew it. I only hoped that the Supreme Commander was able to escape the barrage before he was pulverized.

Instead of explosions however, I heard the sound of laughter. I looked up from my mud soaked pool, to see the Antarean Supreme Commander splitting his sides.

"Don't worry—" he gasped between gales, "We have defensive shields."

Unperturbed I surveyed the situation with my keen politician's eye. Picking myself off the ground, I brushed off the mud and water and smiled, "Just testing to see if this planet has Earth-normal gravity or not." The Supreme Commander blinked in astonishment. "It does." I assured him.

From behind us, through the ground recently cratered by the artillery barrage, seven figures appeared and pointed several pointy sticks in our direction.

"Ulp." said the Antarean. "Ion blasters."

Being the consummate diplomat I was, I ignored the weapons and instead greeted them with what I hoped would be a non-threatening gesture of friendship and respect.

"Take us to your leader." I said.

*

The crimson humanoids led us through the sodden battlefield and into a maze of trenches and bunkers. All the while we traveled in silence.

"It could be worse." The Supreme Commander said in an attempt to calm my nerves, "We haven't been eaten yet."

I looked at my lagomorphic companion. "Does that happen to Antareans often?"

His pink nose twitched in irritation.

"More than you wish to know."

The remainder of our trek I spent in contemplation. From what Fluffy had told me, the Red Cassiopeians called the singular planetary satellite home. If they were here with the heavy weapons and machines I was seeing, then this had to be their beachhead.

Or they had already wiped out the Blue Cassiopeians.

We were brought before who I assumed must be the commander on the scene. He was a large, robust man dressed in a red uniform, who seemed to have a intensely commanding presence.

"Don't worry." The Supreme Commander said, "We sell weapons to them all the time. They wouldn't risk doing anything to us."

I only nodded my mute agreement.

"Almighty General..." The Supreme Commander began.

"Silence!" the General bellowed. "You are an Antarean. You," he pointed to me, "I do not know. You however..." he glared at Fluffy, "You are a liar and thief!"

"Me?" the supreme command squeaked in an effort to appear frightened, "I don't have the foggiest..."

"You sell weapons to the Blues. You lie when you say only the Reds may buy weapons from you. You sell to both!"

I elbowed the Supreme Commander, "You sold to both sides in a war?"

He shrugged nervously, "Who knew they'd stop killing each other long enough to find out?"

"For such betrayals you have been convicted." the General continued, "And sentenced to death." The guards pulled their pointy sticks again.

"Pardon me General." I said quietly, "May we appeal

this?"

The General paused, and glared at me.

"Take them to the Kirk. they will get appeal there."

I felt rather proud of myself as we were manhandled out of the warren of tunnels and towards the surface. "It can't be all bad if were being taken to a church for an appeal." I said positively.

The Supreme Commander rolled his eyes.

"You have no idea."

*

One truly can't comprehend Human influence until one has seen its awesome might demonstrated in the most magnificent way possible.

I didn't understand that until we were brought before the Kirk.

The Kirk was large, and stunningly built; obviously an object of worship by these people. Even more stunning was that despite—or perhaps because of— the garish gold uniform the Kirk wore, he bore a remarkable resemblance to a rather infamous actor I remembered from my youth.

I was so floored at seeing a 60's television icon, I fell to my knees. The Cassiopeians seemed to take this as a sign of my conversion, and they too fell prostrate before the Kirk. He smiled benevolently and placed a hand on my shoulders.

"You may stand." the Kirk said haltingly. "I have no need of your worship."

I was awed. "Are you Human?" even the skin tone was perfect. All that spoiled the illusion was the obvious hair piece.

The Kirk shook his head, "No, I am not wholly human like yourself." he smiled, "A long time ago the Kirk came to us on radio waves from your world, and taught us the way. Both the Blues and ourselves follow the Kirk's way, and the chief amongst each of our races holds the title Kirk to honor the Kirk."

I nodded. It made sense. "Then why the war? Doesn't the Kirk advocate peace?"

"Amongst other thing." the Kirk said nodding, "Most

holy of commands are to destroy all computers and procreate with many aliens." he looked at me, "Have you any human females?"

I raised an eyebrow, "Cassiopeia need women?"

The Kirk only grinned. Not having received a sufficient answer to my previous question, I forged ahead, "About this war..."

"It's a private little war." the Kirk said, "Don't concern yourself Mister. I've decided that since you are human, in tribute to the Kirk, you and your pet may depart unmolested." With that the Kirk turned to the General and promptly ignored us.

"Dammit, I'm a rabbit, not a pet." the Supreme Commander grumbles as we took our leave. Just before we reached the door, he paused and looked back.

"One thing I've been wondering." he said to me, "Do you know why the chief of the Red Cassiopeians wears a gold tunic rather than red? it doesn't make sense."

Before I could answer the room exploded into action as a dozen Blue Cassiopeian commandos leapt from their hiding places and attacked the Red Cassiopeians. The General jumped in front of his leader and was instantly vaporized, leaving behind a small scrap of red velour and a smudge mark on the tile.

"That's why." I yelled to Fluffy as we dove for cover.

In seconds it was all over. The Red Kirk had been captured by the blue troops, leaving us to wonder how we could sneak away. I was proposing matter transportation when a shadow loomed over us.

I looked up to see a much older Kirk standing over our hiding place.

"You are the Blue Kirk I presume?" I asked.

"I am the only Kirk!" the Cassiopeians said as we were dragged from our bolt hole. "Soon these heretics shall be put to death, and there shall be but one Kirk."

I said the only thing I could.

"Fascinating."

*

I was brought before the two Kirks, a pointy stick in the small of my back. Despite Fluffy's discreet gestures for silence, I asked the question that was on my mind.

"Am I correct in assuming then that this war began because both the Blue and Red sides wished to be Kirk?"

Both Cassiopeians nodded, "Come on." Red Kirk said, "Who would want to be Spock?"

"Far too logical." said Blue Kirk.

"May I point out that this war is against the Kirk's philosophy?" I asked.

"Yes." said Blue Kirk with a grin, "But it is not the only human television show we've seen. My people are big fans of the Battlestar."

"Galactica?" I asked.

"Yes!" cried Red Kirk, "Mine too!"

"I see." I said, a plan suddenly dawning, "Then you realize that a very important human holiday is tomorrow."

"Oh?" they asked in unison. "What?"

"Christmas of course." I said.

"Christmas?" they echoed, much as I had expected. I smiled and stepped away from my guards. I mounted a low wooden platform and stepped into a small pool of light.

"Surely you know of Christmas." I said, "It is a time of peace and brotherhood." My mind was racing for other cult television reference, when I hit upon it.

If they had watched television at all, they would remember this. It was my last, best hope for peace.

*

"...and they were so afraid. But the angel of the Lord said, "Fear not, for I bring you tidings of great joy. Today, in the city of David is born a child, and he is Christ the king."

My monologue met with great applause from both Kirks.

"Merry Christmas Charlie Brown!" they cried, embracing each other. "I'm sorry for the misunderstanding. Here, I'll let you be Kirk today."

"No, you can be Kirk today."

"No, I insist."

"No, I insist."

I helped the Supreme Commander off the floor and we began walking out of the cathedral. The Kirks would work things out, I was sure of it.

"Wait!"

I paused as the two middle-aged Cassiopeians ran over to me. "We wish to give you a present." the Red Kirk said.

"Yes." the Blue Kirk said, "For ending our war."

"You see." The Red Kirk said, "You aren't the only human on Eta Cassiopeia. You don't need to spend Christmas alone."

"Oh?" I asked raising an eyebrow.

"Come." the Red Kirk said, "He's been here for a while."

It was the best Christmas gift I could have asked for.

*

The Supreme Commander and I left a few days later. The Kirks had begun arguing about who was allowed to be the Picard and why the Picard should be the Chief among Cassiopeians. As this was an argument I didn't wish to listen to, Fluffy and I decided speed was of the essence.

It was with tearful farewells that we left Eta Cassiopeia. I hated leaving behind a world so infatuated with humanity's greatest art form, and Fluffy hated leaving such a wonderful market for illegal weapons.

And Elvis? Well, Elvis hated to see us go, if only because it ensured he would have to watch Star Trek for another thirty years.

At least he wasn't forced to wear red.

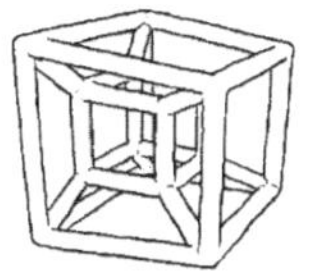

PLAYING STICK

In the beginning there was only darkness.

Then the pool hall opened and we all piled in, ordered a few beer, and started to play a bit of stick. Outside, the primeval night was as cold and black as—night. I hadn't invented Hell yet.

Inside it was warm and primitive drum beats were pounding out of the juke box. I was busy waiting for Gordie, and was having a hard time racking up the table, mainly because the cue ball was missing.

"Dammit." I cursed and dropped on all fours to look for it under the table. A swift kick to my posterior indicated that my partner, Gordie, had arrived.

"Whatcha looking for Stan?" He asked, as he unpacked his stick. I picked myself off the floor and glared at him.

"The cue ball's missing." I said.

Gordie shrugged, and pulled a small white sphere from his pocket. "You wanna use this?"

I took it from him, "Cue ball?"

He shrugged, "I think so. Found it lying around the house." he poked it, "It hasn't hatched yet, so I guess it's safe to use. It looks dead."

I rolled my eyes, "You said that about the last cue ball." I placed the orb on the green velvet table, and racked up the rest of the balls. "You can break." I said.

Gordie nodded, and lined up the cue. I whistled at a passing waitress as he took his shot. With a crack, his stick snapped, and the cue ball flew off the table and onto the floor.

"Scratch." I said, grinning.

"You did that on purpose!" he glared at me. I shrugged and bent to pick up the cue ball. With a start, I realized it was shrinking.

"Dammit Gordie, this thing's hatching."

Gordie walked over and watched it. It was about the size of a pea now, and growing smaller. Within seconds it had disappeared.

"There it goes." I said, and covered my eyes.

Gordie grinned, "Let there be light."

There was a flash, and cursing as the other patrons shielded their eyes from the glare. Gordie grinned stupidly as our eyesight returned.

"Look." he said, pointing at the slowly expanding ball, "My very own universe." I rolled my eyes.

"Moron." I said, picking up the basketball sized object. "What are you doing letting these damned things breed at you place?" I shook my head, "You know this one'll have several baby-universes before it collapses again. They're like rats."

Gordie smiled and shrugged.

The ball jiggled in my hands, and I peered inside the beach-ball sized orb, "I think there's life forming on a planet in there." I pointed to the small blue world orbiting a yellow star, "See?"

Gordie grabbed the sphere and rattled it. He stuck his

face to the thin membrane, and breathed inside. The universe he held swirled. "I am the one true Gord!" he said, laughing hysterically.

"Look, Stan, they're worshipping me!"

I rolled my eyes. "Put it away, and let's get back to playing our game, okay?"

Gordie sighed, and put the universe aside, picking up his pool cue instead. "Can I break again?" he asked.

I nodded, and shot a glance at the still expanding universe. Later that evening, while Gordie was off in the bathroom praying to the porcelain god, I picked up the universe and looked into it. I wondered what it would be like to play with these evolving creatures. A tempting thought. I poked my finger through the membrane, and prodded the little blue world. The tiny creatures went into a frenzy. Already, I had games I wanted to play with them. It might take a while, but then again, they were complex games.

After all, the Devil's in the details...

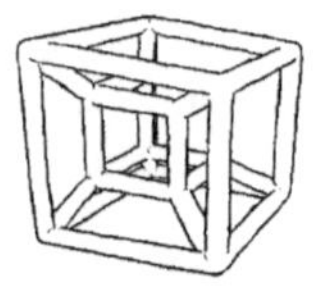

CGXA: 1001
An Introduction to Comparative Galactic Xeno-Sociological Archeology

Good afternoon class, please take you seats. As most of you who have attended the last fifteen sessions know, this course's final exam will be held next session. Accordingly, I have set aside this session as a review and question and answer period. Please hold all questions—that includes you too, Mister Garm—until we have completed the review.

"This course is, of course, an introduction to Comparative Galactic Xeno-Sociological Archeology. By definition we have looked at a broad range of topics as they pertain to several of the major extinct galactic races..."

"Um, excuse me professor."

"Yes, Mister Garm?"

"What about Humans?"

"What about Humans, Mister Garm?"

"In the last fifteen sessions we've looked at Badouras, Nimeritites, Gulapanags, and others, yet we've not done any investigation into Humans. A large portion of our current vocabulary has been traced back to Human languages, and yet, there's no indication as to where they went, or even how they disappeared. Why?"

"I'm not sure I understand the question, Mister Garm."

"Has any investigation been done into the disappearance of the Human race?"

"Yes. Now, as I was saying, the intent of this course has been to study the sociological aspects of—Yes, Mister Garm? Another question?"

"Yes sir."

"Well?"

"Could you elaborate on your answer sir?"

"What answer Mister Garm?"

"About the humans. You said an investigation has been done into their disappearance."

"So I did."

"Uh, could you elaborate sir?"

"Of course, Mister Garm. Some fifty cycles ago a team of pre-eminent Xeno-Sociological Archeologists, including a young graduate student who now stands before you, traveled to the Sol system to investigate the home world of the Human Race, who had disappeared without a trace some sixty-odd cycles before."

"What did you find, Sir?"

"A dead world, Mister Garm."

"My most humble apologies, sir, but was any useful information found to explain the disappearance?"

"Why are you so fascinated by this subject Garm?"

"I have an interest in your career sir."

"You do?"

"Yes sir. In the four cycles you were a graduate student, you worked on three major archeological projects: The Floring Belt Project, the B'lek-tha Project and the Sol Project. In that time you wrote two papers, both published in Galactic Xeno-Sociological Archeology Letters. You have never published a paper on your work on the Humans."

"Get to the point, Mister Garm."

"Why did you never publish on the Humans?"

"Let me ask you a question, Mister Garm."

"Yes, sir?"

"Why do you think the Humans disappeared?"

"Well, sir, the Humans were an important, if somewhat reclusive race. They made several significant contributions to Galactic Culture and science before their abrupt disappearance over 100 cycles ago. There are still rumors that the Humans went slightly mad—some flaw in their genetic structure—and attempted to leave the galaxy."

"I'm less interested in stories Garm, and more in what evidence you seem to think you've recovered."

"Yes sir. From my reading about the era in question, it seems to me that there is some credibility to the madness story. The Humans seemed to be acting more and more erratic, and even more reclusive and insular then they were known for."

"Was there a reason, mister Garm?"

"Yes sir. The Humans were approaching their 'fourth millennium.' Human history has shown a preponderance for group madness upon the dawn of one of these 'New Millenniums.' Perhaps in such group madness, the Humans departed, or even committed mass suicide?"

"Would there be any indication as to why a 'new millennium' would cause such reactions, Mister Garm?"

"No sir. The Human concept of a Millennium, and when a new one comes, is entirely arbitrary. Would it have some sort of biological trigger? Would a Human millennium start when a large proportion of Humankind became mentally unstable?"

"Interesting theory, and a possible explanation for their behavior. The Human disappearance, however was not mass suicide, although it was indirectly caused by the 'Millennium Madness.'"

"Sir?"

"You must understand, Garm, we'd been watching the Humans and studying them for some time. We knew of this madness, and had hoped that we may cure it once Humanity joined civilization. We had also prepared ourselves for the eventuality that we could not cure them, and the entire race went mad."

"There was no cure?"

"No Mister Garm, there wasn't. We watched Humanity approach this New millennium of theirs, and listened as thousands of their kind advocated war, mass murder and suicide and preached the coming of an apocalypse. We did all we could to curb it, but it soon became clear, that the entire race would need to be exterminated to prevent the spread of the disease to other cultures."

"Then Humanity's disappearance was no natural extinction, but a case of genocide for the greater good?"

"Yes."

"I understand. In that case, I would not expect this course to cover Humanity. One last question Professor."

"Yes, Mister Garm?"

"If Humanity's extinction was not a natural event, why did an archeological expedition travel to Sol seventy cycles after the Disappearance?"

"Why, Mister Garm, I'm surprised you haven't guess that already.

"We had to make sure they were all dead, of course."

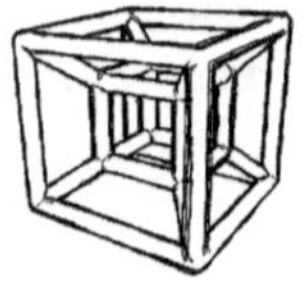

LEST WE FORGET
(published as "The Memory of Death")

This was not the way it was supposed to happen.

Of all the moronic ways to go, stepping off the curb in front of a bus had to be the worst. It was sheer stupidity with a dash of hubris tossed in. Sure, he was invisible to the un-Awakened masses of humanity, but that didn't mean he was any less vulnerable to ten tons of flying metal.

Of course he was immortal, so the bus didn't kill him. It just hurt like the devil.

It had also stripped him of every memory of who he was, and what he was doing here. In the hospital, the nurses would list him as John Doe.

His real name was Death.

Only, he couldn't remember that.

*

It was a dreary and wet November day in Wolfbridge. Mildred Mossey slowly worked her way up the stairs to her apartment. As she climbed, she silently cursed the rainy weather that made her joints ache and caused her arthritis to flare up. She silently cursed the government for not giving her enough of a pension to afford to live in a place with an elevator, and she silently cursed her dead husband for bringing up three worthless children who cared less for their mother than they did for a stray cat.

As she opened the numerous locks to her apartment, she admonished herself for the last thought. The children did care more for her than a stray cat. They sent her letters at Christmas. Form letters.

The apartment was small and rundown. Despite that, she tried her best to keep it as clean and neat as this slum could get. Mildred unpacked the small bag of groceries she had bought and placed them in her near-empty cupboards. Even Mother Hubbard had more. Thank god Mildred didn't own a dog.

She looked out the window as the rain streamed down. The sodden people of the streets shuffled on with their business. More than likely there would be a mugging here tonight, or a murder. Mildred locked her door again, making sure nothing large could get in.

You could never be too careful.

*

"His vital signs are stable Doctor." The nurse shook her head in confusion, "He was hit by a bus?"

The doctor nodded, "So they tell me. I can't see how. He's either the luckiest man in Wolfbridge," he scratched his head, "or a virtual immortal."

The nurse shrugged, "He's got multiple lacerations and some bruises, but no fractures, or anything more than a minor concussion."

The doctor nodded, "Let me know when he wakes up."

"Yes sir."

*

It would normally have been her last day on earth, but she got lucky.

She didn't see the mugger until he jumped out of the alleyway and grabbed her. She tried to scream, but his knife was pressed to her throat, and she could smell her own fear. He took her money, her purse, her briefcase. He then plunged his knife into her throat and, with a grin, twisted and pulled.

She couldn't remember just how long she lay there in the alleyway bleeding her life out onto the pavement, but eventually she came to with a start. She was freezing, and weak, but sheer fear drove her to her feet and to the nearest bus shelter.

When she arrived at the hospital, the doctors couldn't believe a woman drained of blood could walk.

*

Mildred smiled as Bernice opened the door. The two women had been close friends for years. Their children had grown up together, and they had been sharing afternoon tea together for almost half a century.

Bernice smiled despite her oxygen mask and invited her old friend in. Mildred helped Bernice to the table, where tea was already set out. The two women sat and talked as they watched the rain streamed down the kitchen window. It seemed to Mildred that it was constantly raining.

As they talked, Mildred watched her old friend. Bernice was slowly getting frailer and frailer. Her illness was sapping the life out of her, and turning a once vital woman into a shell.

Long ago Bernice had said she would welcome death.

*

He looked around and shook his head, hoping to clear some of the fogginess that resided there. He was in a hospital. Something told him he'd been in hospitals before, on business.

What business?

He shrugged mentally. His memory would come back eventually. There was always time. After all, weren't the only sure things in life taxes and death?

The emergency room was going insane. Doctor Phelps had seen nights where it seemed like the entire city had been shot, stabbed, or mugged; but this, this was completely nuts. He'd spent his entire night treating people who, by all rights, should have been dead.

Phelps shook his head; it was crazy. This shift no one, no matter how serious their injury, had died.

It was absolutely insane.

Phelps brushed a lock of sweat-laden hair from his eyes and glanced at the patients stacked up like cord wood in the waiting area. In his haste to help the next in need, he failed to notice the amnesiac patient wander out of the elevator and into the chaotic ward. Looking slightly confused, John Doe peered at the faces of the injured and the dying.

The last thought gave the forgetful man pause. For an instant, something seemed to jar loose in his memory. He flailed about, grasping for that fleeting instant where the most important thing in the world were the dead and dying.

The security guards were relatively gentle when they sedated him.

*

The tall man dressed all in black looked up from Bernice's composed body. Mildred knew who he was, and why he had come. The smile Bernice had left behind was all the proof Mildred needed. Her friend was gone to a peace greater than she had known in life.

"Thank you." Mildred said to the stranger.

He nodded silently. As Mildred watched, he placed a small object within his jacket and turned towards the door. At the threshold he paused however, and turned back, a small smile on his face.

"Thank you for the hospitality," he said with a wink. "I'll be around this time next year for another business trip."

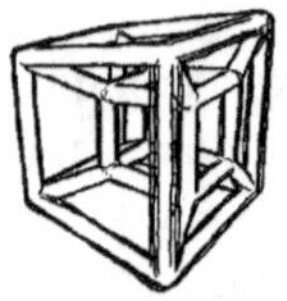

BAKEMONO

The wind screamed across the chasm like a wild thing. A stench like rotted flesh, faint yet pungent, was carried aloft. It assaulted Minobu's senses, but stoically he ignored it.

The ancient wooden bridge creaked and groaned in the wind's assault. Gusts plucked at his kimono and whipped sand and dust into his face. Beside him he heard the boy shuffle his feet.

The cries of the unseen bakemono could be heard from across the chasm. They rose and fell with the wind, but never faded. The dark things that waited in torment on the far side of the bridge knew that their jailer stood across from them. Their torment redoubled, they struck back with the only weapon they had, their wails of agony.

Minobu turned to look at his son.

Not yet twelve, the boy carried himself as if he were

centuries older. The boy watched in fascination as the shadows moved and danced on the other side of the chasm. He watched as they played out their misery and their torment.

"Do not stare too long unto the far side." Minobu admonished, "Fascination and yearning is a door to the soul that they will exploit. Weakness cannot be shown by the Guardian of the Bridge."

Hiro bowed to his father's wisdom. "One day I shall stand here as you do Father." he said with a gravity that belied his youth, "I shall stand and defend the valley from the bakemono."

Minobu nodded, pride swelling his heart.

"Yes." he whispered, "One day the bridge shall be yours."

*

The wind moaned through the open window like a restless ghost. Minobu laid down his brush and walked to the tiny window in his cell.

Behind him a gust disturbed the papers on the floor, scattering them like leaves. A single sheet of rice paper blew across the floor to come to rest at Minobu's feet, its ink smeared.

Fall of autumn leaves
Too soon are cloaked in white
Long, twilight struggle

Minobu knelt to pick up the paper as the door to his cell opened. The monk who entered paused and held out twin swords reverently, "You daisho, Lord Nishimura."

Minobu nodded silently, still bent.

"It is time."

As Minobu straightened, a single tear fell to splash onto the still wet haiku. Accepting the swords, Nishimura Minobu turned and left the cell which had been his home for nearly fifteen years.

His life as a monk was ended.

*

He left the monastery much the same as he had entered it. A tired, broken old warrior, standing on the road between the ancient monastery, and the Shinotsuke Valley below. Autumn had come, and a hint of snow was carried on the mountain winds, yet below the valley was bathed in sunlight, its virgin rice fields glittering in the noonday sun.

Three people awaited him on the path.

"Konichi-wa Otosan." said the man with a deep bow, "I hope the Lord Nishimura is well?"

Minobu bowed in return. "Hai. Domo arigato." he turned to embrace the woman and the child she carried in her arms, "And how is my daughter and her husband."

The man bowed again, "We are well, thanks to the Lord's favor."

Minobu smiled, "Straighten yourself Shin. I have asked you here for a reason."

Shin straightened, and Minobu began the long walk down the mountain path, indicating they should follow. After some time traveling in silence Minobu spoke once more.

"I have had disturbing dreams of the fate of my son." he said quietly, "I fear he is in danger from the bakemono. Should he be possessed or killed, there would be no Nishimura heir. The Five Families rule the Shinotsuke by the Dragon's Law, yet there must be five, or the balance is destroyed. If house Nishimura is to fall, there will be none to guard the Bridge."

A chilled silence underlined the gravity of the situation. Shin nodded, "It is your duty to ensure the bakemono remain across the chasm."

"Yes, giri. My family's duty." Minobu said quietly, "But now my son is in danger, and I have no heir." Lord Nishimura paused and looked at the three before him, "Hidoshi Shin, I ask that you and my daughter return to house Nishimura."

Shin bowed, for he could not meet the Lord's eyes, "Iie Tono. That is impossible. I am heir to my father's house."

"Your father has other heirs. I have only you and my daughter."

"No." for the first time his daughter, Omi, spoke. She held out the small girl-child she carried and who had been quiet for all this time, "You have another." Omi said, "Your granddaughter, Shinobu."

Without argument, Minobu bowed to the wisdom of his daughter's choice.

"Raise her as you would your own daughter Hidoshi Shin, but ensure she is given the tattoo of House Nishimura when she comes of age. Teach her the ways of the valley's power, for I fear she shall be all that can stop the horror my son will unleash."

Shin bowed as his wife wept silently. "Where do you go now, Tono?"

Minobu looked across the valley and to the western mountains where the sun was already setting. "I go to find my son." he took the swords from the belt of his kimono and handed them to Shin, "This daisho shall be Shinobu's when she comes of age. Take care of it, and take care of her.

"She is the last Nishimura, Shin."

Saying no more, Nishimura Minobu walked into the gathering dusk, never to see his daughter's husband again.

*

It had taken Minobu several weeks to travel across the valley on his pilgrimage to the western darkness. For much of the time he traveled unnoticed; one more crazy beggar-pilgrim seeking refuge against winter's impending grip.

It had taken Minobu several weeks to reach the final traveler's hut on the western road. Beyond this the road wound through the mountains toward the bridge and the imprisoned bakemono. No traveler, sane or insane, dared such paths for any reason.

It was late autumn now, and the harvest was in from the fields. Soon snow would race down the mountains to envelop the valley, and both man and beast would stay close to huddled warmth and safety. The icy bareness of winter was when the bakemono were most powerful, and when the Guardian of the Bridge needed the most faith in his duty and honor.

Minobu knew now he was too late. He had failed.

Snow on mountain wind

Valley trembles before storm
A warrior's shame

His arrival would come too late to stop his son from an act of treason. Minobu cursed his own weakness. It should have been he standing against the bakemono on that bridge, and not his son.

Fifteen years. Minobu should have seen it earlier.

If he had not been immune to the bakemono's whispers, how could he ever have expected his son to be?

*

The wind screamed across the chasm like a wild thing. A stench like rotted flesh, faint yet pungent, was carried aloft. It assaulted Minobu's senses, but stoically he ignored it.

The ancient wooden bridge creaked and groaned in the wind's assault. Gusts plucked at his kimono and whipped snow into his face. Across from him stood a man cast in shadow. The shadow spoke.

"Hello father."

Minobu's eyes were steeled, and his heart cold. He had prayed to the Gods that Hiro might have the will to resist, might have stayed on the eastern end of the bridge.

He had not.

Now the man Minobu faced was hardly recognizable as his son, Hiro.

"You have changed, Father." The shadow said.

Minobu said nothing.

"I too have changed in fifteen years." The shadow approached, and Minobu could see the red flame of hatred burning in the young man's eyes.

"Hiro." the name was torn from Minobu's lips.

The shadow laughed. "I am Hiro no more, old man."

"Then what are you?" Minobu whispered.

"What you made me." the shadow said as it approached, and began to cross the bridge. "What the bakemono offered to make me after I was abandoned by my father. The fools."

Minobu took a step backwards as the shadow continued across the bridge. A aura of crackling energy seemed to appear about the young man's hands, drawn from the rocks and plants about him.   Beside Minobu, a hardy mountain evergreen withered and died, its life drawn into the maelstrom.

"No."   Minobu cried against the rising winds, "You cannot!"

The shadow paused and laughed, and allowed the energy to die away, "You are correct, of course Father.   The bakemono gave me the power to draw upon life itself, but never realized I would use it to enslave them to my will. Why then would I waste it killing you?"

"Hiro." Minobu gasped as the shadow staked him, "Please. This is my shame; a stain on my honor."

"I am not Hiro!" the shadow cried, "I am Shugenja-Kami, Sorcerer-King, and I will not let you take your own life Father! I will have the satisfaction of killing you myself!"

Shugenja-Kami leapt from the bridge, a katana suddenly in his hands. Knowing the strike would split his skull, Minobu knelt to receive the death-blow.

There was a loud crash of steel, and a shower of sparks, and Minobu lived. Stunned the warrior staggered to his knees, his daughter's gentle hands assisting him, her whispers in his ear.

"Omi?" he croaked.

"Oh, how lovely." Shugenja-Kami gloated, "My sister has come to help her father."

Omi said nothing, and moved to impose herself between her father, and the man who had once been her brother. "I am the least of your worries." she whispered with hatred, "There is another Nishimura, and she will ensure you will not enslave the Valley forever."

Shugenja-Kami frowned in consternation, "Another?"

Minobu stood, "Yes, another Nishimura."

"Tell me where she is." Shugenja-Kami demanded coldly. Minobu's eyes grew hard as he gathered the remains of his courage. He stepped in front of Omi, staying her hand, her words on his lips.

"Never." Minobu said quietly, "She is safe where you can

never find her."

Shugenja-Kami's scream of rage echoed among the snow-capped peaks. Suddenly all was still and silent.

"Tell me, or do not; it is of no matter." Shugenja-Kami said with finality, "Good-bye sister."

Instantly he crossed the gap between them, and with a flick of his wrist, it was over. The daisho clattered from Omi's nerveless fingers to the snow covered stones, as her head tumbled into the chasm below.

Minobu stood there, knowing he had failed utterly. His family was dead. His son was possessed by the bakemono—controlled them. Soon enough a dark horde would descend upon the Shinotsuke Valley and destroy it. A horde led by a Nishimura.

Minobu could no longer contain his grief and shame.

"Weep not, old man." Shugenja-Kami gloated, "Your life shall end soon enough."

"Yes." Minobu whispered, "But your sister shall see your doom. The dragon will devour you as you wish to devour the valley."

"I have no sister." the Shugenja-Kami chuckled, "Not any longer."

"But you do." Minobu insisted bitterly, "She is the last Nishimura."

"Then I have little to fear." Shugenja-Kami scoffed.

"Not for another thousand years, perhaps." Minobu said, "But she will come to you, and you will pay for your betrayal of the Five Families."

"It is of no matter." the Katana flashed in the blood-red sunset.

For Minobu, the pain was mercifully brief.

*

The moon was rising over the eastern mountains, and the wind had fallen to a low moan. The cries of the bakemono grew still and silent. They sensed that their new master would soon release them from their torment.

Shugenja-Kami smiled as he stood over the corpses.

They would be released soon enough. He would see to the deaths of the Samurai and the rest of the Five Families. With their demise, the Valley, and its power, would be his.

A small gust of wind tugged at a piece of rice paper that protruded from inside Minobu's blood-stained kimono. Shugenja-Kami plucked it from the remains. The ink was smeared with blood and snow, but the haiku remained readable.

> *Ice flashes like steel*
> *Moon glows in night's darkness*
> *Tears on crimson snow*

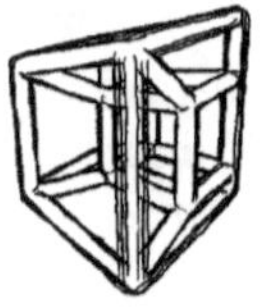

LOOKING INTO PARADOX

The floor was as cold as death.

Naomi felt the chill burn into her cheek. She felt its numbness leech the warmth from her body. She knew that if she didn't get up soon, she may well die, frozen to the floor.

Why so cold? The question—was it spoken aloud?—seemed to ring through the metal caverns, like a sigh in a morgue's silence.

Naomi opened her eyes, dreading what she would find. There, mere feet away lay the dead, unstaring eyes of one of paradox's victims. Beyond the frozen corpse, lay the shimmering blackness of Paradox.

Yet it was the glazed-over eyes which drew Naomi's attention. She knew those eyes; she had plumed their depths on more than one occasion.

They were her eyes.

*

Pulling herself off the floor was almost the hardest thing Naomi had ever done. Harder still had been the task of dragging her own corpse across the floor and into a side laboratory. There it lay, under a plastic sheet, atop one of the workbenches. Moving it—moving her—was probably a futile gesture, but Naomi felt the need to respect the dead.

Even if it was her own corpse.

Now though, the question remained.

What had gone wrong?

Fragments of memory bobbed like flotsam upon her consciousness. The experiment was proceeding nominally until the power spike, and then all hell broke loose.

Naomi looked about what remained of the complex. The control room was destroyed, so too several of the other labs. The only rooms not wholly blocked by fallen steel and rock were the lab she was currently in, and The Pit.

The Pit. The area in which paradox was to be evoked; mankind's first attempt to breach the space-time continuum on a local basis. The Pit; where she had found her corpse.

Had she died there?

Will she die there?

Naomi shook her head to clear it. What was the point in asking such questions. Survey the situation and then deal with what you find.

What was left?

Ventilation; air was still being pumped into the complex. Power; some of the dangling conduits still sparked with a live current. Computers? Most likely. Paradox seemed stable enough, and that could only be with the control of the master Cray.

There was, however, no exit. Even if she had access to the airlocks, the pressure suits and emergency bubbles were apparently buried under tons of rock. Half the complex had collapsed when Tokamak Three red-lined.

What could she do?

Damned little. There had been no wireless transmitters in the complex for security reasons, and the OC3 landline was most likely cut; not that she would have access to the feeds, since the control room and all the redundants were gone too. She had maybe twenty-four hours of recycled oxygen before the carbon-monoxide levels became lethal. There was no hope of rescue before then.

That left her one last question.

What had gone wrong?

*

Death and dying was a constant in the life of a flight surgeon. Naomi was no stranger to any of it. She'd headed the forensic investigation after the Armstrong Dome disaster.

"It's your talent," her father once said, "to cut frogs open and figure out what made them croak." They had both laughed at the remarkably bad pun. Naomi wasn't laughing any more.

"Subject shows no signs of carbon-monoxide exposure beyond normal, trace levels." Naomi paused in her examination, suddenly looking away. Of the thirty-odd cadavers entombed in the complex, only one was intact enough to provide the answers she needed. Even so...

It had to be a first; doing an autopsy on yourself.

"There are indications of blunt force trauma to the posterior cranium." No one would ever hear the recording, but for posterity's sake, Naomi wanted to keep the tremor out of her voice. "The impact caused massive hemorrhaging within the brain. Death would have been almost instantaneous." Thank God for small mercies.

Suddenly, a fragment of memory surfaced.

Jose had been in the Pit when the first tremor was felt. She rushed in to help free him from a fallen girder when the second tremor struck. that was when Paradox flared black. Screams. A cry of despair beside her. Her cry. A glimpse of honey-blond as she was pushed from behind. A scream; falling metal? Human? Something else? Then, blackness and cold.

Naomi shook herself from the fugue.

"What happened here?" she whispered, but the corpse was as cold and unanswering as paradox itself.

What happened here?

*

It was a hard thing to wait for death. As the hours passed, Naomi busied herself in what little there was of an investigation. She knew that if she paused, even for a moment, the crushing realization of what awaited her would descend.

Better she stay busy until the end.

Yet there seemed to be no answers. Even her doppelgänger provided no clues to why the paradox had flared, or what had caused the massive destruction. It was clear the paradox was the culprit—there were consequences to tearing at the universe's fabric—yet the equations had indicated opening paradox would be safe. they had been right, hadn't they?

Naomi knew little about quantum physics or higher-order math. From what her colleagues had told her, paradox had something to do with string theory and other dimensions curled up into the normal four. Naomi was the flight surgeon—the medic for chrissakes—how would she know if the equations were wrong, or of the equipment had failed?

Yet doubt gnawed at her. Surely, somewhere in the wreckage, there was a computer log of those last fatal moments. Maybe, in plumbing the computer's depths she could find the answers she needed. Would she find what she sought?

She would.

Hidden under a small pile of crumpled metal and crushed stone, lay one of the primary data recorders. It contained a precise log of the events leading up to, and following paradox.

Leaving her dissected corpse behind, Naomi dragged the recorder to the only functioning data terminal. Across from her, still confined to a corner of The Pit, paradox awaited.

*

The concept was simple: create a tear in the local space-time continuum, stabilize it and see if the laws of relativity could be circumvented. According to the equations, such a tear—such a paradox—would allow theoretical faster-than-light travel between any two such portals. The portal you emerged from was dependent upon both an object's velocity and angle in relation to the tear at the moment of entry.

Using those equations, engineers had spent years building devices to harness the power used to create a paradox. Massive computers were designed to compute the variables, with legions of programmers coding the applications that would bring paradox into being.

Somewhere, in the midst of those trillions of lines of code, a single mistake was made. A mistake that could only be found under specific conditions; conditions present in the formation of paradox.

A plus sign had been transposed with a minus sign. A small mis-calibration had been caused by the error, and a tiny amount of energy leaked into paradox, and leaked back out.

Three-tenths of a millisecond earlier.

*

For the want of a nail...

Naomi shook her head in utter disbelief. No one had seen the implications. No one had realized that if an object could travel faster than light, it could also travel backwards through time.

Paradox was a time machine. it seemed so simple.

Less than a joule of energy had arced into paradox when it was torn open. The velocity had been low, the angle shallow. The energy had arced back out of paradox milliseconds in the past, upsetting the finely tuned instrumentation and causing a feedback loop that overloaded Tokamak Three. The explosion had destroyed the complex, killing everyone inside.

But it didn't have to happen!

Naomi glanced over her shoulder at the obsidian enigma. Paradox sat as still and silent as ever. Devices and computers buried deep in the bedrock kept it functioning, at least until the other three tokamaks failed in a thousand years. Here it would sit, long after she was dead, a failed time-machine forever trapped under miles of rock.

But it didn't have to happen!

If she could calculate it properly, she might be able to send a message to the past; to explain the error and keep them from creating this future. She could stop the catastrophe; save everyone here. No one had to die.

Yet, she had nothing to transmit with. there was no way to send a message to the past, unless she found a way to carry it herself.

Naomi looked at paradox once more.

Unless she could carry it herself.

*

The air was getting bad. She could feel the muzziness seeping into her brain, carried by the carbon-monoxide that was poisoning her atmosphere. No matter, she would be leaving soon enough.

What if this doesn't work? Naomi shook her head. If it didn't work, so be it. She had tried her damnedest to prevent the tragedy.

<u>What if it hasn't worked already?</u> That was a more disturbing thought. Perhaps she had failed, and that was why she had died in the past—unable to warn her fellows of the danger paradox posed. No, there was something not right about that.

Naomi took a final look at the data the dying computers had generated for her. She would have to act fast once on the other side. She had only seconds to halt the experiment before the catastrophe occurred. Naomi looked at paradox. She needed to be as precise as possible when entering, otherwise she would fail to react the right place at the right time.

What if I've already failed?

Refusing to listen to doubt, Naomi screwed her eyes shut, and leapt into the darkness.

*

Screams rang in her ears. Her eyes snapped open, and once more she relived the horror of those fatal minutes. The floor shook as the second tremor from the tokamak's explosion struck.

There, in front of her, the thin blond woman in the flight

suit knelt before a prostrate form. Naomi stumbled towards the figure.

Have to warn them.

Above her the girders shrieked their distress. Soon this whole place would collapse. The disaster had already happened. Naomi had failed.

Yet there was still hope. Maybe if she went back to the future she could try again. no. She had failed once. What if she was stuck in a never-ending loop of failures—trying to make it back to warn her friends.

The floor shifted, and the blond woman tumbled into Naomi's arms. She found herself once more staring into her own eyes.

This time had been different.

Yes. When she'd done the autopsy, she'd found no traces of carbon-monoxide. Surely her own tissues were saturated, but her future-self's hadn't been. Now, this time, things had changed again.

Maybe there is a chance.

In that instant of realization, Naomi pushed the blond woman—her younger doppelgänger—towards paradox. The groaning of metal was louder now, but Naomi screamed to herself over the din.

"Go back! Stop this!"

Somewhere above her the screams were silenced by what sounded like a clap of thunder. It was as if the entire world fell onto Naomi, crushing her beneath its weight.

Things were different this time.

The doppelgänger staggered backwards and was enveloped by the shimmering ebony of paradox. All about her Naomi could feel the complex and its inhabitants die.

All but paradox. It would wait for her next attempt.

Things were different this time.

Naomi smiled, and let the darkness claim her.

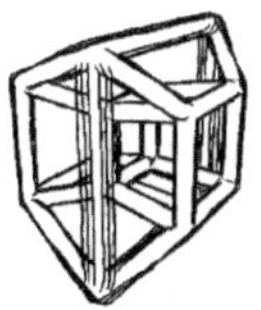

PEACEMAKER

The guns' roar was so loud it had been heard across known space. The roar reverberated in Lord Nerul's palace—its terrifying sound shaking his soul.

"Such a travesty." he whispered, looking across the moon-spattered garden. Behind him the door opened, and the roar's echoes began.

"You wished to see me m'Lord?"

"Ah, Sir Meldrick, do come in and have a seat."

The younger man entered the room and took the proffered seat. He relaxed slightly as he settled into the plush chair. Lord Nerul smiled.

"If I may ask, m'Lord, why have you summoned me?" Meldrick asked after a moment's silence.

"You've heard of the Arcturan Situation, of course."

"Of course."

Nerul sneered, "The bloody barbarians are slaughtering each other." He paused as he saw Meldrick's almost-hidden grimace. "My apologies Meldrick."

"No offense taken, Lord."

"Nevertheless, this is exactly why I asked you here."

"Lord?"

Nerul smiled and sat down across from his young guest, "I am told they say you're the greatest leader of men since Caesar; the greatest warrior to grace the battlefield in a hundred years. In your short career, you've never failed a mission and never lost a battle. You have a tenacity and a self-confidence my other officers lack."

"They say it's my heritage."

"Genetics and upbringing are only part of it." Nerul said, suddenly stiff, "Bloody Hell, Meldrick, in this day and age, war should be a thing of the past. Yet we still have these dangerous child-races gnawing at our borders, or at each other. Humanity should be above this."

"We haven't been at war in three centuries."

"Police actions, peacekeeping, pah." Nerul scoffed, "Pretty word for what we know is limited warfare." he glared at the young man, "People like the Arcturan's revel in the filth and blood. The violence is like a drug isn't it?"

"I wouldn't know sir."

"They're your people."

"My mother's people."

"You were raised among them, you know how they think. They made you the warrior that you are. They bred you for what you do." Nerul paused for breath, "Meldrick, I need you to go there and do what needs to be done."

"You're sending me to stop a war?"

"To keep the peace." Nerul smiled, "But I'm sending the entire Terran military under your command. We will crush this war, and every other one. We will make the peace, by force if need be. Arcturus will be the first, but soon the other barbarians will fall in line."

The First Lord of Terra picked up a pen from his desk and from a drawer pull a sheet of parchment. "You will be the greatest Terran hero to ever live, Meldrick. Together we can end this foolishness. Think of it, peace in our time."

The half-breed officer bit back his reply, and watched as Lord Nerul signed the declaration. With a stroke of his pen, he would decree the end of war. By his order, the guns would fall silent, never to roar again.

Once Meldrick had left, Nerul stayed to watch the moonlight play across his garden. In the sky above, tiny points of light danced as the might of the Terran military was shuttled into orbit for their final campaign. The flares of the fusion engines made a pretty backdrop against the Geneva night. It was hard to imagine they had been designed to transport murderers.

Soon enough, that would end. There would be peace in his time. Mankind would herald him as a hero—the Peacemaker.

A female voice called for him from the palace. Nerul smiled and went inside.

Elsewhere, the guns roared.

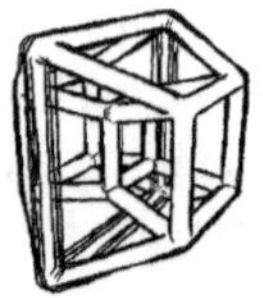

PEACEKEEPER

The guns had fallen silent. Across the bloody battlefield that had once been Arcturus, all was quiet.

"The Peacekeeper comes."

It was a whisper on ever Arcturan's lips.

It was a curse.

*

What have we done here?

From a balcony of the Council Building Sir Rufus Meldrick looked out across the city. Randolf, the Arcturan capital, was less damaged than most of the planet's other urban areas, yet even it showed the scars of a ten year civil war.

What have we done?

Throughout the streets Meldrick could see his soldiers—all

members of the Terran League Armed Forces—standing guard; keeping the peace. It was dusk, and curfew had fallen. In Randolf, the Terran soldiers owned the night. Elsewhere, it was no so peaceful. Yet Meldrick's mandate stood: Pacify Arcturus. Bring peace, even if by force.

What have we done to this place?

The question rang in his ears, and Meldrick didn't know if he meant the Terrans, or the Arcturans.

*

He had grown up here. His mother was Arcturan, a free trader until that night, thirty years ago, when she was raped by three Terran soldiers on leave. Meldrick never knew his father—his mother never knew which of the rapists had fathered him—and if he had, he would have killed the man himself. There had been no need however, the local's had dealt with the three men. Meldrick had been born half a year later, somewhat premature. His survival had indicated to his uncles that he was a warrior, and that was how he'd been raised.

When Meldrick turned eighteen, he joined the TLAF. That had been before the League had abandoned Arcturus.

Now the League wanted the planet and her people back, but on its terms. Peace. The end of war.

Meldrick had come home. He wished he didn't feel like a rapist.

*

The command center was dim and filled with a haze. Meldrick ducked in, and squeezed past two Terran Marines. Their face plates were mirrored, but he knew the looks of disgust they wore; he could feel it.

"General." His aide, Nemoch, saluted. Meldrick waved him off and peered at the tactical display.

"Trouble?"

Nemoch grinned, "You could say that. We've disarmed most of the Loyalist forces on Gai'th'in, but some of the most militant have barricaded themselves on the southern part of the continent, and are shooting at everything that moves."

"What do they have?"

"A brigade of armor, some nukes, but I doubt any air power or transport."

"Nukes?" That concerned Meldrick.

"Yeah, old fissionables. Bloody indig scum just love to blow shit—" Nemoch trailed off.

"Yes, they do, don't they?" Meldrick's voice was cold. "Who do we have in the local?"

"The Seventeenth ACC."

Meldrick frowned. "Get me out there, I want to mount with them."

"Sir!" Nemoch's tone was hushed, "The Seventeenth is the most bloody, xenophobic unit of the whole damned army. Half of 'em would sooner kill you as look at you."

"I know." Meldrick's eyes were aflame, "Which is why I want their command."

"It's your funeral." Nemoch said with a shrug, but Meldrick only nodded.

"So be it."

*

Thirteen years ago southern Gai'th'in had been a lush agricultural belt—the bread basket of Arcturus. Now it lay in ruins, a testimony to the savagery of the civil war.

The sun, red and bloated, peered down upon the dusty waste, ignoring the suffering of the Terrans unused to the heat. While most of the officers and men had stripped out of their uniforms to avoid heatstroke, Meldrick stood reveling under the sun. He had been tempered in the blazing heat of Arcturan summers, and, like his people, was used to the searing noonday sun.

It was the hatred that radiated from the troops that burned him.

"I'm sending the entire Terran military under your command. We will crush this war, and every other one. We will make the peace, by force if need be. Arcturus will be the first, but soon the other barbarians will fall in line—think of it, peace in our time."

First Lord Nerul's words seemed to echo across the wastelands. It was at Nerul's behest that Meldrick stood here, ready to lead a Corps of crack soldiers against a brigade of Arcturan rabble. A thousand men awaited Meldrick's inspiring words. A thousand pairs of eyes pierced him with their loathing. Meldrick had spent his entire career leading men into battle—he had never lost.

Yet now he was not the invincible hero. No, instead he was a half-breed Arcturan. No matter what he said now, that would never change. Nemoch turned and nodded to him, indicating that it was time for his speech. Meldrick sighed and mounted the stage.

"We go now to secure peace on this world. We go to lay down our lives for the Terran League, but also for more. We go to fight for peace, to ensure peace, and to end war. It is the First Lord's dream, and mine as well. We shall see the end of war. There will be peace in our time!"

A ragged cheer rose from the gathered soldiers, but Meldrick could tell their heart wasn't in it.

Neither was his.

*

There was hatred in the Arcturan eyes that followed the tanks. Meldrick's armored column wove through the narrow streets of Ecredale, the largest surviving town in southern Gai'th'in. From shattered building the hostility radiated like a palpable force.

The Arcturan people hated Meldrick as much as his own men.

Truth be told, Meldrick hated himself. He hated himself for pandering to the Terrans, for following their lead and subjugating his people. He hated himself for wanting to side with his people, and for his desire to abandon his duty here, and take up arms against those who would rape his world. He hated himself for being torn by conflicting duties.

From the ruins of what must have been the government center, a small man appeared. He strode into the street, weaving between the rubble, to interpose himself in front of

Meldrick's lead tank.

"Halt." Meldrick ordered. The column of armored vehicles pulled to a stop. Nemoch took his place in the commander's cup, manning the heavy power gun as Meldrick dismounted and stepped towards the small, balding man

"You are not welcome here." the Arcturan said, "Your Terran Army is not welcome here, and you, half-breed, aren't welcome either."

Meldrick nodded, "I understand, nevertheless, I have a mission to complete."

"You understand?" the other man scoffed, "Understand that we don't need your morality or your peace. We can find peace on our own terms. We have a right to determine our own fate. We don't need some coward without the stomach to fight ordering us about."

Meldrick laughed, "Is this wreckage peace on your own terms?"

"Maybe if you hadn't abandoned your people, you'd know."

"I cannot leave."

"We will not let you stay."

Meldrick's eyes narrowed, "Then you will have to kill me."

"So be it."

Before he could reply, Meldrick heard the high-pitched scream of falling shells. He closed his eyes, knowing he had walked into the most obvious of traps. For the first time in his life, he tasted defeat. From the sky, death rained, and each of the falling projectiles seemed to curse his name.

"Peacekeeper!"

The universe seemed consumed in the roar of hatred.

*

It was Nemoch who found him under the collapsed wall. The man's head was swaddled in blood soaked bandages, and he wore a grim look of determination. Meldrick winced, less at the pain, and more because of the other's appearance—and his own shame.

"It's over." Nemoch said as he helped the medics move Meldrick from the rubble and to a waiting stretcher, "Despite the ambush, we were able to crush the local opposition. We lost eighty-three men."

"And the Loyalists?" Meldrick croaked.

"Wiped out to a man." there was a hint of glee in Nemoch's cold eyes.

Meldrick looked away, a tear streaking the blood and dirt on his face. Beside him he could hear the whine of a activated pistol. he turned back, to see Nemoch leveling his service weapon.

"Why?" Meldrick asked, "Not simply because I'm a half-breed?"

"No." Nemoch whispered, "For the treachery that killed eighty-three of my people, and because you would never allow us to finish this mission as it should be finished. With your death, we will crush these barbarians, and make the peace."

Meldrick nodded regretfully. There could be peacekeepers, only when there was peace to keep.

The gun roared.

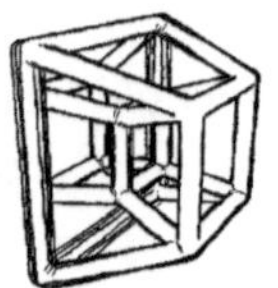

INNOCENCE

The sky shook over his head, and he curled up tighter against the driving rain. As the thunder rolled again, he squeezed his eyes tightly, trying not to be frightened, trying to remember what the sergeant had told him. The mud pooled about his feet and he wiped it from his rifle, wishing he were home with his mother. It was warm and dry at home—not like the mud and damp he always seemed to have to slog through.

Home was…soft. Gentle. At his mother's apartment in the Arcology there were plants and pets and music--sometimes even dancing if some of the neighbors came to visit. He had never liked dancing very much—that was more his sister's thing, but she had died on a battlefield like this one a solar year ago.

Or was it two solar years ago?

He sniffled silently, so used to the smell of death that he didn't notice the stench anymore. All around him the rest of his unit prepared for the enemy's next attack. So intent were they on their objective, the air seemed to hum in anticipation-- like a violin string suddenly plucked.

Out of the sky the shells began to rain, throwing up dirt and flinging human bodies about like rag dolls. He squeezed his eyes tightly again, ignoring the screams. His objective was to hold this trench line.

Not one step back—that's what the General had said.

Hold the line--no matter the cost.

Shrapnel sliced through one of the soldiers beside him and she screamed as her Exo was torn apart. It was a scream that was brutally choked off as another shell fell.

Had his sister screamed like that?

His tears were lost amidst the rain as it pelted his face.

*

Several miles away the General watched his units move on the holographic display. His face was set in stone as the battle ebbed and flowed before him. Not for the first time the General marveled at just how bloodless it all seemed when viewed this way. He could almost forget that there were real people dying out there.

One of the holographic icons blipped out.

Impersonally, the General noted it. Another position had been overrun; the line was weakening. Soon the enemy would break through into his rear areas. Grimly he exhaled and ground the butt of his cigarette into the deck plate. The smoky haze hung around him like a halo. His staff were waiting for him to make the decision that would win this battle--perhaps even the war.

Could he dare greatly?

Was offense the best defense?

He closed his eyes, and images of battle flooded back to

him. He remembered the blood, the horror, the mutilated bodies.

The General shuddered. He gently touched the scar behind his right ear, where his battle implant had been and made his decision.

"Order the troops to engage with Exos."

He opened his eyes, wishing there were another way.

He felt like he was sending his children out to slaughter.

*

In the trenches the soldiers heard the orders as they were passed along the battle line by the sergeants. In his trench--crouched among the dead and the mud--he turned on the power pack of his Exo just as he had been instructed.

The exoskeleton came to life, and he felt the flex of its artificial bones and muscles. He felt the pressure the machine brought to bear on his frame and ground his teeth as the familiar wave of pain and nausea passed.

An Exo's pilot took terrible punishment as the powerful machine used his flesh as a supporting framework. It was the flexibility of youth that protected the pilot of an Exo. An adult would be crippled, where a child was merely injured. They would heal the damage that would shatter older bodies.

It was a bitter gift.

All around him the members of his unit waited for the order to attack the enemy. The rain pelted him, making him cold and miserable. Once again, he longed for the sun-drenched garden in the Arcology where he grew up. Most of all he wanted to stop being afraid.

Beside him Joey was whispering something under his breath. Some of the boys felt the power of the Exos and it went to their heads. Some of those boys weren't afraid; they were the schoolyard bullies who liked the feeling of power the Exo gave them.

But Joey was his friend.

Joey was like him.

Afraid.

Moving towards Joey, he had to step over the corpse of a

former comrade. So many of them lay still in the muck that surrounded them.

"It's bad." Joey said quietly.

The reply was a silent nod. In the distance they could both hear the enemy's movements. The shelling stopped, leaving an eerie quiet hanging in the air. Even the thunder had subsided. It was like the calm before a storm.

Their comms buzzed to life.

The attack order was given.

*

The General watched as his little holographic soldiers leapt from their positions to engage the enemy units. There was little he could do as he watched the icons waver and blink out. Some enemy icons disappeared, but far too many remained.

At heart, the General was not philosophical. He had been a soldier for most of his life and was by definition a pragmatist. Yet it was the sight of this sanitized mass-murder that tore an anguished question from his soul.

Why?

Why was man, of all creatures, so inclined to war against his neighbor? Why was mankind so driven to kill his neighbor and his neighbor's children? Why was it Humanity's children that fought these wars?

Was it glory? Power? Mere survival?

Another icon flared out of existence.

The General's soldiers were only twelve years old.

*

The reasons for the war had become hazy over time. Some said it was a war of survival--that the enemy had descended from the sky to harvest resources; oil perhaps, gold or water? Others claimed the enemy was interested in Humans as a source of protein.

The loudest droned on about how victory would uplift Humanity--would prove those made in God's image were superior to all other life in the universe. It was a Holy War you see.

There were some very quiet voices who said the war had started because Humans had been arrogant and cruel to those it discovered were alien in more than just skin colour or culture. The war--according to the quiet voices--was penance for the pain and hate Humanity had delivered unjustly upon the enemy. Indeed, some whispered that Humanity had created the enemy itself by its own actions.

Most however said nothing about the war.

Those were the people who feared a knock on their door asking for their children to come to the recruiting center. It was all voluntary of course—after all, why would a patriotic family not be willing to fight for Humanity?

Worse yet were the knocks that came later--those followed by grand speeches about heroics and sacrifice. Those that left the parent with a small box as the only memory of their child--if they got even that.

The broken people--they likely spoke the most truth about the war. They spoke about it being a monster separate from the Enemy that stalked Humanity's children. This monster called War consumed only blood and treasure, leaving nothing of value behind.

These broken voices were often those found by the children who had served but served no longer. Perhaps they spoke a truth because they had lived it--because they understood the war.

They were no longer children however--because what child can truly comprehend war?

*

On the field, the enemy was slowly winning. He and Joey had bounded out of their trench when the order was given, and quickly moved across the scarred and torn wasteland.

They were both driven by fear. In their twelve years, neither of them had faced such horror. In training it had been a game. A game like Tag or Ninja. A game wasn't real. When you killed someone, they counted to five and jumped back up.

A game wasn't real. You couldn't die in a game.

As they crossed the barren land, grotesque forms rose in

the distance. The enemy's bloated, white Exos were a mass of artificial muscle and sinew enveloping a pressure suit.

Once visual contact was made both sides laid down a hail of fire. The terrain exploded in gouts of dirt and filth as it was churned into a morass of mud and bone and death.

Few survived the slaughter without some wound.

Some of the deepest wounds you couldn't even see.

*

Joey had told him once about the life his family spoke about, from before the war. Few of the soldiers knew anything but the war, but Joey's parents had him late in life--after their other children had left home. His parents had owned a farm--a vast acreage of wheat and barley which became fields of gold during the harvest. It had been a hard life--one reason why Joey's older siblings had left the farm once old enough--but for his parents there was pride in their accomplishments; pride that their hard work fed others.

Then came the war.

At first it seemed that nothing changed very much--the war was far away at the edges of Humanity's exploration. But it escalated and grew closer. One of Joey's siblings had enlisted. Later, another was drafted.

Neither would end up returning to the farm.

Taxes went up, revenues collapsed. Eventually the government took the farm because they couldn't trust Joey's parents to grow enough grain.

Then came the bombings. After that, there was no farm.

When Joey had been born, his parents lived in one of the Outland Arcologies--the same as most everyone's parents these days.

They still dreamed about the farm.

Joey had always wondered why.

What was the value in a field of gold?

*

The General, like his men, had been taken from his family at the age of ten. By then, the war had been raging for several years, and the enemy's technology had given them the edge.

115

Two years before his enlistment, however, the General's people had stolen the design for the Exo.

The Exo was the ultimate weapon of war.

Its advent would change the face of combat. It turned a soldier into a walking arsenal. Its bristling array of weapons could ensure victory, or at the very least, survival, for the General's people.

Massive artificial muscles drove pistons and gears that carried the heaviest of weapons and armour almost as thick as that of an ancient battleship--or so the soldiers claimed while talking between themselves. These days there were so many different manufacturers and so many different types, the soldiers often chided and joshed each other over which one was better. Did you have a PowerMAX Type 82? Well, my Obentoid Mk III could clearly beat that in the ring. It was all a joke.

The other joke was that they were simple enough to use, even an adult could do it.

Sadly, while true, it still required a child to operate it safely.

While an adult could pilot an Exo, the strain on their frame invariably caused chronic damage. Over time it would shatter bones, crush organs and cause damage to the central nervous system. Eventually the user would become a crippled husk.

Children, though, were young and resilient. They could grow into the punishment the Exo exacted on their body. Their flexibility and youth would protect them from the worst damage. Anything the Exo could dish out to its pilot could heal with enough time and therap--so long as it was before adolescence was over.

Few worried about the years of therapy they would need when they mustered out.

Few lived long enough to muster out.

The General remembered his training. It had been brutal, but he had survived. He had been one of the best Exo pilots until he was wounded at Al-i-Bhatain. It was there that an enemy particle blast burned and irradiated him. Maimed and delirious from the pain he had lain on the battlefield for a standard day before he had been discovered--Humanity had become so used to having no survivors left after combat, it was often assumed that every casualty was a KIA.

They had found him however--but strength of will alone had not been enough to allow him to survive until his rescue--it was the thought of his mother; of the pain his death would cause her that kept him clinging to hope.

He was her only child. His birth had nearly killed her--he couldn't let his death finish the job.

Months of recovery lay ahead of him; months where his thoughts continually returned to what he had done wrong--why his friends had died. He worked tirelessly studying the Enemy's movements and tactics to distill what their strategy might be.

He wanted to ready to fight the bastards and extract some payback when he was back on his feet and into the field.

But that wasn't going to happen.

Deemed unfit for field duty, he had been promoted to where he could use his experience to command the battlefield. Now unable to have offspring of his own, the General saw those soldiers as his children. They carried his legacy into combat. So the General's children would face the enemy, fighting for their race's survival.

They would face the enemy and die.

*

He was still at Joey's side when they leapt into the crater to attack the enemy soldiers. Using his smaller stature, he dodged the enemy's clumsy slash and stabbed his opponent with his knife. The tungsten blade bit deep into the artificial muscle of his opponent's Exo. In response, the enemy lashed out with its blade. A vicious strike sent him sprawling.

The impact jarred him and set his ears ringing. A sharp pain in his knee told him that one of the Exo's joints had been destroyed. He looked at the stump of what had once been his leg and felt a wave of nausea flood through him. The Exo's life support system sensed the blood loss and injected drugs to stabilize his condition and cauterize the wound. Already he felt their numbing effect as they worked to sedate him. His thoughts became unfocused.

Where was the enemy?

The enemy soldier moved in to finish off its oblivious target. Joey called out and raised his weapon.

The enemy turned and fired.

*

The enemy had broken through the line in several places, and the General had scrambled all his available reserves to try and plug the gaps. Hopefully, they could withdraw in good order without taking additional losses. The battle here was a massive defeat, but he couldn't allow it to become a rout.

As he gave his orders the General wondered if his people would survive, or would they become just another page in history; conquered by a greater force?

He sighed, knowing that at sixteen he had become an old man. How much of him had died on the battlefield that fateful day he was crippled? How much of his mother's son was left?

Perhaps too much.

Onward he would have to drive his soldiers--harder each time to try and steal a step from the enemy. He would need to become harder if Humanity were to survive.

Yes, the General would have to become harder.

The soldiers would have to become harder.

*

The battle had passed him by, moving further to the south, leaving him in the mud and water of the shell crater. He ignored his throbbing leg as he cradled Joey's head in his lap. Across the crater his opponent's lay crumpled in a heap. A nameless and faceless enemy in life, the soldier remained so in death. All that remained were its helmet and pressure suit. His weapons had vaporized the rest.

He remembered a fleeting image in his mind's eye of the creature's death as its skin boiled away——but none of the soldiers could remember anyone ever having seen one of the enemy soldiers outside of their Exos. Most claimed they had tentacles and little chittering claws where their teeth should be. Some claimed the Enemy had one eye--others said dozens.

Perhaps there are different Enemies under their Exo suits-- lots of different species working together to exterminate all humans.

It didn't really matter. You kill the enemy or it killed you. It didn't matter what it looked like or smelled like or how it screamed as you blistered its flesh.

For you to live, the Enemy had to die.

He was cold, sitting there in the mud. The cold crept into his body as he rocked Joey's corpse. The cold crept into his heart as he sat in the bloody water of the crater weeping over his friend.

His eyes streamed with bitter tears. All life had fled those eyes, leaving them as dull as Joey's. He had done his duty. He had killed the enemy. He had paid the price. But it wasn't enough.

He had still died, even though his body would continue to live. Soon enough he would have to kill again; but perhaps it would be easier the next time.

And easier the time after that.

And the time after that.

*

The rain fell, unabated and uncaring. The grey clouds ignored the weeping boy below as coldly as they ignored the dead and dying on both sides of the battle. The rain was eternal. The clouds were immortal.

Below them, children died in agony as childhoods were brutally slain by their enemies, and their own General.

Some of the dead could even walk off this battlefield.

Innocence would not.

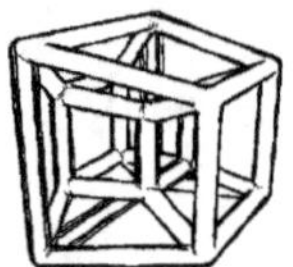

SILENCE OF THE CROATAN

The **Croatan** hung above them as they descended to the verdant planet below. Like seed pods shed from a flower, each of them hoped to bloom in the freedom their new home promised.

Misha drew Rachel to him and pointed to the green and brown land masses that floated quietly in a sapphire sea.

"There's Samuel and Anubis." He said, indicating the twin continents with his finger, "We're scheduled to make land fall on Anubis. There's a small bay on the north part of the continent, not far from a native settlement." The colonist grinned at his wife. "This is everything we've wanted."

Rachel nodded, tears glistening on her cheeks.

"We can finally learn to live with nature again." she said, wiping the wetness from her face, "The natives will teach us all we've forgotten."

The pods glowed as they entered the atmosphere.

*

They called themselves The Children of the Sky. As such their entire culture was focused on the sky, and it's wonders. Omas knew as he saw the pods fall from their seed-ship that change was coming to his people.

Many seasons ago other men came from the sky, and looked about Omas' world. They seemed pleased with what they saw, and spoke often of wishing they could stay and 'relearn the old ways' from Omas' people. They did not stay, but Omas knew that they would someday return. The Sky had told him.

Omas knew change was coming, and prepared his people.

*

Misha looked up when he heard Omas enter. The colonist smiled warmly and offered his friend a seat, "Omas! How provides the Sky this day?"

Omas sat, his face carved in stone, "The Sky provides both sun and rain." The native greeting was becoming common within the colonist's vocabulary, Misha thought. Misha called to his wife to bring some refreshments, and sat back, observing his native guest.

Omas was short and thin, and would have passed as an adolescent human, were it not for the age that showed in his eyes. They were ancient eyes. Misha never could tell how old any of the natives were.

"So, old friend, how may I help you?"

Omas bowed his head, "I bide in conversation with my brother Misha." he said, "If you are occupied, however, I will return at a better time."

Misha laughed, "I'm in no hurry. Two years here have taught me not to hurry. After all," he winked at Omas, "When have your people hurried for anything?"

Omas nodded, "My people do not hurry. Haste is of no consequence when the Sky opens and closes." He paused, his sharp eyes boring into Misha, "Why do you believe you need be like my people?"

Misha sighed, this was becoming too frequent a conversation between him and Omas, "My people come from a world where there are so many of us, we can't count them all. My world has been stripped bare of trees, and fields and rivers, by the growing hoard. We colonists sought a new world, a simple world."

Again Omas nodded, "So your seed-ship came here, and your people were planted in the rich soil of my world. You are welcome here. I again ask you, why must you be different people, by trying to become like my people?"

"Your life is simple, and uncomplicated Omas." Misha said watching Rachel enter the room, tray in hand, "That is what I want for us and our children." He placed a hand on his wife's enlarged belly, and smiled.

"I understand." Omas said simply. "Soon, you too shall understand the ways of my people."

Rachel beamed, "Does this mean your Chief has decided to let us take part in one of your ceremonies?" Omas shook his head.

"Not our Chief." he paused, "For two seasons you have been among us, watching and waiting to become like us. Soon the Sky shall allow you your chance." He reached out and touched Rachel, "When the child is to be born, the Sky shall give you the gift you seek."

A shrill electronic signal interrupted the native. Misha cursed and leapt to his feet. Running to the corner of the room, he slapped a small switch on his transceiver. He looked up and grinned sheepishly, "Sorry about that. The Croatan's sending us its daily report."

"Your ship?" Omas said, pointing to the ceiling, "That circles this world?"

Rachel nodded, "It speaks to us every day, telling us what is happening on the planet, and sometimes tells us about what is happening at home."

"On other worlds?" Omas asked thoughtfully.

Misha nodded, "We talk to other worlds, through the

<u>Croatan</u>, and they talk back to us. It's a relay station for the colony."

Rachel beamed proudly, "The only technology we have here, and we don't really need it." she squeezed Misha's hand, "Sometimes engineers can be too sentimental about their technology."

Omas stood, "Will this ship speak forever?"

Misha laughed, "No, not forever. One day we won't need it anymore. Then we'll order it out of orbit, and scuttle it someplace safe."

Satisfied, Omas left.

*

The sky was overcast and threatening rain as the sixty-four colonists wound their way down the steep canyon sides to the valley floor below. Misha helped his expectant wife as they carefully followed the well-worn path. With them were thirty other couples, each expecting the birth of their first child. Omas had made it clear that only the pregnant colonists and their mates would be allowed to take part in this ceremony.

Rachel paused to rest on a large boulder, and through a break in the clouds Misha pointed out a small, bright star.

"The Croatan." He said, and chuckled, "It'll pass over here every forty minutes. And I thought you could only see it on clear nights." His smile faded as he saw Rachel shiver in the cold wind. He took off his wind breaker and wrapped it around his wife's bare shoulders.

"I thought Omas said it would be a nice night." Rachel said through chattering teeth, as Misha helped her to her feet, "I'm freezing in this summer dress."

"Hopefully, it'll be warmer inside." Misha said.

Rachel nodded, and suddenly grimaced in pain. Misha gripped her tightly to keep her from stumbling, "The baby?" he asked, worried. She nodded and then cried out as the labor pains struck again.

All about them the cries of other expectant mothers were filling the air. The sky flashed, and a deep bass rumble signaled the coming of a storm. Before them a small figure appeared on the windswept path.

"Come!" Omas cried against the rising winds, "It is nearly time!" he waved the colonists forward, as other natives appeared to assist them to the bottom. "We must hurry!"

The sky opened, and it began to rain.

*

Rachel and the rest of the women were laid upon stone tablets under the open sky. The rain was falling heavier now, but the wind had dropped off to a soft moan. Misha shivered in his wet clothes, his wife's hand clenching his.

The native attending Rachel looked up, "Soon now."

Another flash of lightning.

Rachel screamed and pushed, bearing down.

Another crash of thunder.

A head appeared.

Misha watched in amazement as his son was born, washed by the sky's driving rains. The native nodded, as he wrapped the child in a small cloth and handed him to Misha.

Rachel was softly moaning as Misha accepted the child. The canyon rang with the cries of mothers in pain, but none of newborns. Misha looked at his son, so beautiful and so perfect. So silent. The child reached out a small hand, and clamped onto his father's finger. Misha smiled as his son opened his eyes.

They were ancient eyes.

In shock Misha turned to his wife, only to find Omas gently closing her eyes. The native straightened and turned his ancient eyes to Misha.

"My wife? My son?" Misha stammered.

Omas nodded gravely. "You wished to become like us." he reached out and took the child from Misha's arms, "You cannot."

Misha looked about, as other stunned colonists stood beneath the sky, their children looking at them with ancient eyes. With a crash, a bolt of lightning lanced out of the sky to strike a small, bright star in the heavens.

"Your children can." Omas said. "You cannot."

Misha screamed his rage at the sky.

*

The wind blew the grasses gently, and a rustling sound broke the silence of the summer's day. Somewhere beyond the hills and fields of the abandoned settlement, children played, but they sang no songs, and they did not laugh.

Their parents were gone now, and perhaps that is why they did not smile. Perhaps that is why their eyes looked so ancient.

The field lay fallow, alone and silent but for ghosts, and small creatures. Rising from the deep grasses was the last monument left by the colonists.

Though covered in moss, the metal still sparkled brightly in the noon day sun. Engraved on the jagged hull plate was a single word.

***Croatan*.**

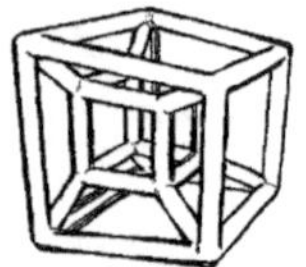

FEARFUL SYMMETRY

There was blood in the water.

Not just a trickle of blood; not a fine pink coloring in the stream, but tendrils of half-coagulated blood. They swirled and danced in the eddies and rushed by in clotted wisps that spoke of recent death.

Ross recoiled in disgust, throwing aside his canteen and looking upstream. From his vantage point he could see a pink fleshy mass jammed against a sunken tree. Distended entrails guided him to the dead creature, half hidden in low hanging branches.

Ross brushed aside the pine needles, to find the mutilated form of a dog. With some trepidation, he knelt in the mud, and examined the corpse. Huge claw marks rent the poor creature's flanks, and it was obvious that powerful jaws had turned its guts into hamburger.

Ross had seen death before, but never like this.

Suddenly alarmed, the hiker quickly gathered up his belongings and made his way back through the darkening woods to his cabin.

The trees no longer seemed to afford shelter.

*

When Corporal Ross MacKinnon was given the opportunity to take a leave of absence from the Canadian Forces, he jumped at the chance. Feeling he had to get away from it all, he packed his meager belongings and headed east, to his family's homestead on Prince Edward Island.

His grandfather had died several years before, leaving Ross a cabin in the woods. The cabin was a half-mile back from the highway that wound across the north-eastern shore of the Island, and with the nearest major town being ten miles distant, Ross felt he could some peace at last.

But while Ross could escape contact with people, he was unable to escape the nightmare visions that plagued him. Each morning the peace was shattered by the screams that propelled him into consciousness.

And try as he might, Ross couldn't wash the blood from his hands.

*

His grandfather had left him twenty-five acres of mixed woodland, and Ross knew every inch of it by heart. He had grown up here; spent his summers curled against nature's unspoiled bosom. Each winter the boy chafed at school and life in the big city, wishing he could be back on the Island with his grandfather. These woods were home.

Yet now the trees seemed somehow taller, and more menacing. The woods grew dark as the sun dipped below the horizon, and Ross was still a quarter-mile from the cabin. he wasn't afraid of getting lost, he knew the trails in these parts like the back of his hand.

He was afraid of whatever killed that dog.

There weren't supposed to be any large predators on the

Island, but whatever had attacked the dog was large, and mean. For the first time in his life, the forest primeval held no joy for Ross, only an unease that haunted him.

Ross wasn't used to being the hunted. He wasn't used to not being totally in control. He needed that control, of himself, of his environment. Security came in knowing the ground you were passing through. Ross no longer knew this ground.

Still several hundred yards from the cabin, Ross paused, and scanned the shadows. He was sure he had heard movement. The telltale rustle of underbrush that spoke of passage.

There was something out there. Something large, and it was pacing him. It moved when he moved, it stopped when he stopped, and it hungered.

Ross could feel its hunger.

Unable to control himself, Ross dashed forward, towards the edge of the woods, towards the cabin. Like liquid darkness a shadow followed him, tiny pricks of light glowing amber with hunger. It flashed through the woods, barely disturbing them with its passage, and as he glanced over his shoulder, Ross could almost see the fluid motion of its supple body. It was a hunter, like him. It was a killer. Like him.

Ross broke from the woods, making a mad dash for the darkened cabin. Behind him the shadow stopped pursuit, and turned back. There was always time later.

Ross didn't stop running until he was inside, a locked door behind him. breathless he dropped his knapsack, as a peel of thunder rolled across the sky.

Outside, it began to rain.

*

Thunder storms could be especially violent where the ocean met the land. Being an island, P.E.I was paradoxically well known for both its calm waters, and violent thunderstorms.

The sheets of lightning throw strobing lights across the cabin, while the sound of thunder shook the pine timbers.

Ross had no television, and his radio was drowned in static from the storm. Chilled, he built a fire in the stone fireplace, and dug a tin of ravioli out of the pantry. Some quick work with the can-opener, and Ross was pouring the pale lumps of pasta into a battered pan hanging over the fire.

A roll of thunder startled him, and he dropped the tin in pain. A small, ragged cut showed where the sharpened edge of the can had nicked him. Blood welled up, and he watched in fascination as drops fell into the embers with a hiss.

Blood and fire. That's how it began wasn't it?

With little reason to stay awake, Ross bandaged his thumb, quickly ate supper, and crawled upstairs and into his bed. The staccato beat of the rain on the roof was somehow soothing, and he drifted off to sleep.

One there, though, he found his nightmare stalked him once more...

*

The nightmare was always the same. Enough reality to make it tangible, but just enough surrealism to scare him shitless and screaming.

It always began with the blood, and the fire.

They were all so young then. It seemed a lifetime ago when he first joined their ranks. ***The Tigers***. The elite of the elite. The best the Canadian Forces had to offer. He wanted that, to be the best. Acceptance was harder than just wanting to be the best, however.

He had to prove he was the best.

In blood. In fire.

No one really knew where the ritual had come from. It was the secret of the regiment—a dark regimental tradition— and the proving ground for new members. Every year the new members of the Regiment would be led to a place of fire, and there pledge to ancient pact.

Ross remembered the night he pledged to the regiment. The moon was full and blood-red. He was led through woods as dark as pitch to the clearing where a fire silently smoldered.

"Are you prepared to pledge your life for us?"

Ross nodded, "Yes."

"Will you commit your soul to us?"

"Yes."

The inquisitor grasped Ross's wrist.

"Do you give your blood for us?"

"Yes." Ross whispered as the firelight flickered across the knife blade. The steel bit into his palm, leaving a crimson trail. He squeezed his fist closed, and watched as the flames leapt up to consume the red drops.

"Do you feel the power?"

Ross nodded, his eyes flashing in the firelight. Deep within him, something awakened. No longer was he only a soldier. He was a hunter, a tiger.

"Do you feel the rage?"

Blood pounded in Ross's ears. The thrumming sounded like ancient drums, and the echoes carried him and sustained him. The rage burned, an angry coal within his belly.

"The fire gives you power. The fire sustains."

Yes.

The drums beat louder, and from the shadows a shape flowed into the pool of light. A sleek, powerful form, its pelt striped in flame and shadow. Fire burned in the tiger's eyes, the same fire that burned in Ross's belly.

There was blood on its ivory fangs.

The drums beat louder.

The tiger leapt.

*

The rain, falling on the roof like drumbeats, was drowned out by his screams. Ross staggered from bed, the bed clothes tangled about his feet. He stumbled and fell, landing heavily on the pine boards.

"No..." he whispered trying to rub the crimson blood from his hands. It stained them, and him with a deep red ochre. Then, with a blink, it was gone.

Had it been there?

Where was he?

Ross blearily looked at the clock. An hour had passed.

The storm still raged outside, and the darkness in the cabin was broken only by the pale red clock face. He picked himself off the floor, and threw the knot of sheets onto his mattress. There he sat beside them, his head in his hands.

The door rattled, and he jumped, startled. Outside the wind howled, rattling the door again. Dismissing the noise, Ross turned away, only to have the door blow open, the wind and rain tearing into the small cabin.

"Shit." Ross cursed, as he stumbled down the stairs. The blowing rain pelted him as he approached the open doorway. A sheet of lightning ripped across the inky sky, and Ross threw his hand up to shield his eyes.

Silhouetted in the doorway was a slender, black figure.

"Ross." the whisper was seductively female.

Blinking away spots, he squinted at her. As graceful as a predator she slinked across the threshold, he ebony skin slick with the rain. He knew her face.

"Surely you remember me, Corporal."

A hand slick with wetness gently caressed his cheek.

It couldn't be her. Ross tried to pull away, but she drew him closer. He shook his head, pleading, trembling in terror as her tongue played across his lips.

"You do remember me." she purred, "Good."

Her eyes flashed with rage, with fire, with blood.

"It wasn't wise to disobey your Masters."

Tearing himself from her sensual grip, Ross stumbled into the rain and the mud. She had to be another hallucination, like the blood. he looked back, and there she stood in the doorway, a black woman, eyes glowing with hatred.

The sky lit up, and for a moment, he could see her, illuminated in all her glory. She smiled, barring her fangs.

"You are the one." Suddenly, she was gone.

Ross sprinted into the woods.

Behind him, the hunter slinked after.

*

Somalia had been a serious fuck up. everyone knew that. It took a while, but eventually the truth of the what had happened over there came out in federal commissions, and courts-martial.

Most of the truth.

When Ross first laid eyes on her, she was already dead. It was early morning, but already flies buzzed around the young woman's corpse. Ross knelt down, placing a hand over her unseeing eyes. The body was cool. this woman had been dead for several hours.

"Okay." He growled at the three men who had led him here, "What the fuck happened?"

"It was Lieutenant Axworthy. He told us to clean her up, and get rid of the body. You know, cover-up." The private looked terrified, "He's an officer and all Corporal, but..." none of these three men wanted to take the fall for this.

Neither did Ross. He bit his lip and surveyed the situation. They were congregated in an abandoned alley near the red-light district. There was no doubt about what had happened. Axworthy was known for enjoying his women submissive and his sex brutal.

She couldn't have been more than nineteen.

Will you commit your soul to us?

Axworthy, like Ross, had pledged on blood and fire. They were all responsible for each other's actions. They all hung together, or they all hung separately. Axworthy was a piece of skinhead trash, but he was a Tiger.

They were both Tigers.

Will you commit your soul to us?

Fuck, if he hadn't already.

"Do what the LT said." Ross turned and left.

The walk to the compound was the longest he'd ever made. The roads were caked in a thick dust that seemed to hang in the air. It lay as a thick, dark veil over the buildings of the compound. The sun burned down accusingly as Ross walked past the sentries and towards the officer barracks.

The dust parted as he stepped into the shade of the building, the air conditioning blowing aside the heat and grit with a wall of cool, chemical tinged air. Taking a deep breath,

Ross strode down the hall.

The steady click of his boots on the floor brought to mind the beat of the drums that night so long ago. He could feel a darkness follow him, growing deeper as he approached Axworthy's quarters. Pausing at the door, Ross looked about him. In the periphery of his vision he could see a shadow, but it disappeared when he looked at it.

His knock echoed hollowly through the deserted corridor.

"Come." a voice rasped from inside.

Ross opened the door and stepped into his nightmare.

"Jesus fucking Christ." he whispered.

The darkness was almost complete, broken only by a dozen candles scattered about the room. in that dim light, strange ichor glistened on the walls. Axworthy, emaciated and covered in angry sores, sat cross-legged in the center of the room. The candles flickered as Ross closed the door. A heady stench of sex and putrefaction hung in the air, and Ross choked down the urge to gag.

Axworthy cackled, his face a death's-head. "Christ doesn't enter into it Ross." he wheezed, his eyes aflame, "I'd not mention that name again, if I were you..." he beckoned with a withered taloned hand, "Come, sit down."

Ross hung back by the door, "What's happening here..."

Axworthy's face fell, and the fire in his eyes dimmed, "A pact we all made..." he coughed, "They came to collect from me, and I could not pay." he looked away, "The price of my desires."

"You killed that girl, didn't you?"

Axworthy nodded, "Yes. They wanted her, but I couldn't help myself." he licked his cracked lips, "I couldn't sacrifice her to the fire. She was so young..." he shrugged, "Then again, I never fucked a nigger girl before."

Ross shuddered, "Who are they?   What are you talking about?"

Axworthy stood, and the shadows seemed to darken, the candles dimmed. "Can you imagine the embodiment of the perfect hunter? A shadow, swift and deadly and beautiful..."

Ross retched as the stench of death struck him. "I don't understand."

"The Tiger." Axworthy whispered, "Driven by rage. the perfect hunter. man, the perfect prey." his eyes glittered with madness, "In the darkness they find us, and play with us, and watch us shiver with fear. They only ask for small sacrifices to their fire. to feed their rage." he pointed to the candles, "It is a small fire, burning within all of us. A dark fire. We made a pact, we were chosen to help feed that fire. To become more perfect hunters."

A chill ran down Ross's spine as he saw something move in the shadows. Twin pinpoints of fire burned brightly, to complement the candles. Axworthy nodded.

"I see you understand now." he shivered, "I have failed, but you can still save yourself. you are the one, now that you've seen them. They are your masters, obey them and you shall have immortality." his voice dropped, "Disobey and you are meat." a manic look came to the dead-man's eyes, and he turned, his arms splayed. "I submit to judgment!"

A scream like the end of the world tore from the shadows, ivory fangs dripping in blood. Ross, unable to tear his eyes from the beast, watched as Axworthy was torn into bloody rags. The beast turned to looked at Ross, and smiled.

"You are the one." it whispered in a sultry voice.

His hands covered in Axworthy's blood, Ross fled.

*

The trees tore at him, their branches like clutching fingers, slowing him down, letting her catch up. he was the one all right. the one to blame. the one to hunt.

Axworthy was dead. The three other men had each gone to Yugoslavia and never returned. One by one, those involved had joined the Pink Mist Society.

Now Ross was next. The one most to blame.

The one to make a pact, and now the one to pay the price.

"No!" Ross screamed his defiance to the alien woods, "I will not lie down! I will not give up! I will not die!"

He stumbled out of the clutches of the woods, and drew

up short against a cliff. Solid ground fell away to the rocks thirty feet below. Whitecaps smashed against the red stone below, slowly tearing at the Island and its shores.

Bleeding, and battered, Ross turned to face the woods, his back to the sea. At the edge of his vision he could see a form pacing amongst the twisted pines. A lithe shadow, waiting for its moment.

"Come one you fucker!" Ross screamed at it. "Take me, if you dare!" he felt the rage burn within him, "Let it end as it began. In blood!"

"And fire?" the whisper was in his ear.

"Oh sweet Jesus..." Ross dodged away, but was too slow. Silver talons ripped under his chin, tearing at his exposed throat.

"Jesus can't save you now." the eyes burned, "You're mine now."

He gurgled and collapsed as a wave of nausea passed over him. Triumph burning in her eyes, she straddled him, her tongue lapping at the blood that pumped from his neck.

"Do you know what he said to her before he strangled the life from that girl?" the hunter purred with pleasure, "He said, 'I never fucked a nigger girl to death before.'"

Ross struggled weakly, his eyes making the pleas his mouth could no longer voice. She only smiled, and shook her head.

"You swore an oath." she said cruelly, "You made a pact with powers beyond your knowledge. Now they own your soul. You played with fire. Now you get burned." her laughter was mocking. "Do you still feel the rage burn?"

Deep inside his belly, the coal of anger and hatred exploded, roaring to life. Enraged, Ross gathered the last of his energy and drew his legs against her chest.

There was a look of shocked pleasure in her eyes as she flew off him, propelled by his legs. Then she plummeted over the embankment, and from view. Long moments later, he could hear a sickening crunch as she struck the rocks below.

His rage drained, Ross allowed the soothing blackness to

take him.

*

The storm had broken by the time he regained consciousness. Dawn was only a few hours away, and with the clouds fading like a dream, a full moon rose above the now quiet ocean.

Ross painfully dragged himself to the edge of the cliff, and looked down. In the pre-dawn light he could see the woman's smashed body splayed across the rocks below. Blood stained the waves that lapped against the corpse.

Haltingly, Ross touched his neck. Where her talons had torn the skin to the bone, there was only tender scar tissue. He was alive.

You made a pact.

I will not die!

Do you still feel the rage burn?

Deep within him he felt the fire burn. He felt the hunger. He stood, his strength returning, and looked about. His rage had transformed him, his hatred a rebirth. The world was changed, and he saw it with new eyes.

He was the hunter again. The beast who would hunt his master's prey. A beast who would hunt his Masters. He was a Tiger.

His eyes flashed with a burning desire.

He was a Tiger, and he had a hunt to begin.

Silently he padded from the open cape, and into the dark woods.

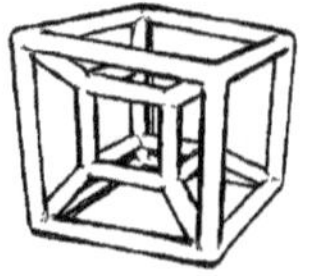

DANCE WITH ME MY MUSE

Once, she could fly.

She would glide through the air, her body held in a graceful sweeping arc. Carried by her gazelle's legs, she would float across the stage to land in her partner's arms. Swift, and lithe, like a cat, she would flow across the stage to rousing applause and standing ovations.

Once, she could fly. Those days were over.

After the accident, she had become an award winning choreographer. The ability to fly, to dance, was no longer in her sleek legs, but the music and the dance were still in her head. Using the spark given her by her muse, she would conduct others in a ballet arranged to her own internal symphony. Later, she taught young dancers the steps and the rhythm of her music, of her muse. her dance studio rang with laughter, music and joy. Through her students she could fly once more.

One day she awoke to find her muse had fled.

Once, she could dance. Those days were over.

*

She sat alone in her studio. Sheets were draped across the unused furniture, and the now silent grand piano. The once polished floor was now dusty with neglect. The lights were off, and only the dim illumination from the street outside allowed her to see in the darkness.

A thin wisp of smoke curled upward from her cigarette. She placed the butt to her mouth and inhaled. The red of the ember lit her face with a hellish glow before fading once again. She exhaled, and watched as the smoke joined the haze that hung in the air.

Standing, she walked to the middle of the floor and cocked her head, as if listening. Raising her arms, she took an experimental spin. With an almost inaudible creak, her knee gave way, and she tumbled gracelessly to the floor.

There she sat for a moment, weeping silently.

"I can't hear it!" she cried, "Why can't I hear the music?" Not expecting an answer, she hung her head in her lap and wept bitterly.

An answer came, unbidden and unexpected.

You have lost a part of you, the shadows seemed to whisper. *That which make you whole. Have you lost your soul?*

"My muse." she said quietly, "It has fled."

No. from the shadows a form was coalescing, merging with the airborne dust and cigarette smoke, creating the specter of a young man. *I have not fled. I am here.*

She scuttled away from him as he offered his hand to her. *Do not be afraid*, the ghostly young man said, *I will not harm you.*

"Who are you?" she asked as she stood up, still backing away. The specter laughed, a sound like summer's rain.

I am that part of you, you have ignored for so long.

"Why are you here?"

To return the music to you. To let you fly once again.

She shook her head, "I must be delusional."

Perhaps. The shadow smiled, *Don't you want the music?*

She nodded vigorously, and he reached out his hand again to her, offering her the last chance she had dreamed of for so long.

May I have this dance?

Her heart in her throat, she took his hand.

*

She flew once more.

With her muse's hands wrapped firmly around her waist, she glided through the air, and across the dance floor as if she were twenty years younger. Years fell away as she felt the strength return to her legs, to her body. Once more she was a gazelle bounding across the dance floor.

She could almost hear the cheers.

And in the background of it all, was the music. Her symphony had returned in all its glory. The music ebbed and flowed with the movements of her body, and she with the movements of the overture.

All the while, supported by her muse.

The music reached its thunderous crescendo, and breathless, she once again touched ground as her muse released her. Energized by her performance, she reached up and took the ghost's face in her hands, pressing her mouth to his.

He returned her kiss with a passion she had lacked for so long. This was her muse, that vital, passionate part of herself. he was the embodiment of the music, the song, the dance.

"Where have you been for so long?" she whispered to him. He smiled down at her, his face wreathed in swirling motes of dust and smoke; like a halo about an angel.

I have always been here. He said.

She shook her head, "I have not."

Through the large windows the dawn was breaking, and sparkling beams of light were inching across the room and reflecting from the mirrors. The scintillating shafts highlighted the dust and smoke that hung in the air, and amidst it all, her muse, triumphant.

She smiled.

We haven't much time. He said. *Your final performance is at hand. It shall be your master work, but we must prepare.*

She nodded, "Yes, I have to choreograph all the moves, prepare the costumes, the props." she smiled up at him, "We shall prepare together."

The specter nodded, *Nothing has changed.*

"No." she said, "Nothing."

*

As the shafts of morning drew shorter, so too did their time. Much needed to be done before her grand performance could take place. In a frenzy the dancer and her ghostly muse set about the final preparations.

"The piece must have dramatic impact." she said as she shimmied out of her dress, "Thus the heroine must be seen as vulnerable."

Yes. the specter nodded.

She tied her hair back and felt the cord's silkiness on the nape of her neck. "Soft." she murmured, "Soft and vulnerable."

Yes. her muse again agreed, *Yet strong and defiant.*

"She must struggle against fate until the end."

The specter nodded.

"Grace is her name, and grace is her hallmark." she said as she pulled the chair to the center of the dance floor, "She sits and awaits her love, but is defiant to the last."

Beautiful. her muse said, *The audience shall weep.*

She paused and looked at herself in the mirror. No longer was she an old, withered woman; she was once more a lean and lithe dancer. She bent and stretched, running her hands across her taut legs, feeling the energy, the magic they hid within. She straightened the simple slip she wore, and took a breath.

"Are we ready?" she asked her muse.

The ghost smiled, *It is time.*

The sun streamed in the windows, its orange and red hues lost in the glare. She stepped onto the chair, her body alive with the pulse of the music. She swayed to its rhythm as she draped the cord over the exposed rafter and tied it off.

The music was reaching its climax once more, when the bright sunlight of morning banished the final shadows from the dusty dance studio.

The snap of the noose echoed through the now silent room. The music was fading as the blood pounded in her ears. She gasped and fought, defiant to the end.

Once again, she could dance.

The ghostly shape of her muse faded away as the shadows disappeared. No longer the form of a young man, it was once again only a cloud of dust and smoke.

In the center of the room, her dancer's legs twitched with the dying spasms of her last masterpiece; her muse's dance. When it was ended, she hung in the air, suspended by only a thin cord.

Once again, she could fly.

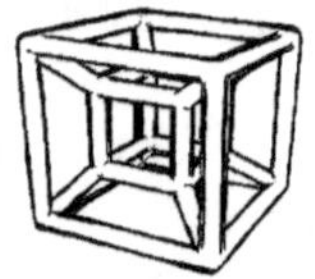

SILENCE TO THE ENDS OF THE EARTH

The switch receded with a click, and she finally understood.

Her whole life she had wondered where she belonged. Forever out of place, she'd flowed with life's currents; flotsam on the stream of time. Where was she going? What would she do? These were questions to which she had no answers, until now.

*

The world was a broken wasteland. She could see the scars left by humanity, the decaying urban-scape that was haunted by the ghosts of all who had died within its bowels. Haunted by all that it had killed.

The sky was opaque. Its poisoned facade the color of shit. Her entire life had lead up to this moment, where she stood amidst the ruins and listened to the ghosts as the passed by.

The noise of their passing was deafening. The screams of the murdered tore through her.

She smiled, knowing that soon, the screams would stop. Peace would reign.

*

In the mind's eye, you could see the joy that lit her face. She had found her purpose. no longer was she a vagabond on life's highway. God had finally spoken to her, and his words had rung true. Clichéd though it may be, she felt his love, like an angel sitting atop her shoulder. His messenger had brought all she needed. Her suffering ended with his spoken words.

"Who are you?"

Your disciple.

"What do you want?"

To change.

"Where are you going?"

To change the world.

"Will you return to the beginning?"

Yes.

*

The weight was almost unbearable. She could stand it though, for a little longer. Standing amidst the wreckage, she smiled, knowing that soon she, and the ghosts would rest. Their torment would end, and in one moment of brightness, she would change the world. Peace. Serenity. Silence.

To the ends of the earth.

With a cry of pure joy, she pressed the switch.

*

Imagine a moment frozen in time. A woman stands alone amidst a sea of humanity. She is of no concern to them as they rush home from their menial jobs. They cannot hear the voices of the dead. They cannot hear the words spoken to the woman. They are drowning in a sea of noise.

The woman's cry shatters the tableau. In a blossom of fire, their world ends.

Sound's fury tears at the wretched city, exorcising its inhabitants. Elsewhere, others are exulting the same joyful chorus. A dozen fires are born in the darkness. A million lives are swallowed by the thunder. Only the echo of their passing remains.

Finally, the dead are silent.

*

It was not the end of the beginning, but the beginning of the end.

From the ends of the earth, all is silence.

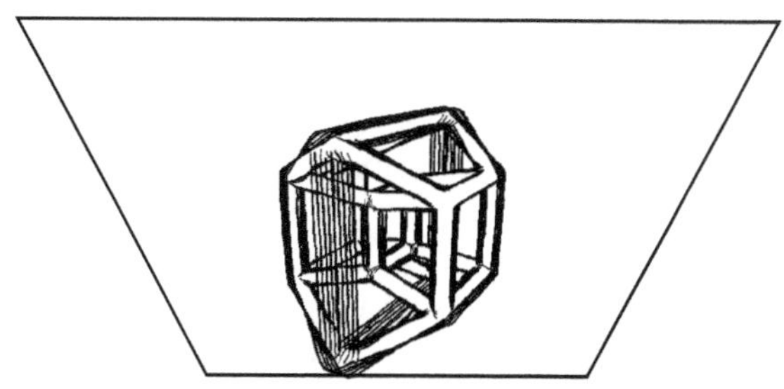

BIBLIOGRAPHY

"Before the Crash," Original to this collection, November 2015

"Second Moon," SpaceWays Weekly, March 1998

"Fatal Error," E-Scape, December 1998

"In a Family Way," Jackhammer, February 1999

"Climbing Over the Fourth Wall," Jackhammer, August 1998

"Movements of Fire and Water," Jackhammer, October 1998 (with Staci Layne Wilson)

"Meiyo No Izou" published as **"Honor's Legacy,"** Jackhammer Print Issue, October 1998

"Yesterday's Footsteps," Jackhammer, May 1998

"Memoirs of an Intergalactic Diplomat," Jackhammer, April 1998; reprinted in SpaceWays Weekly, April 1999; reprinted in The Best of the Web Anthology, June 1999

"Shined, Sealed and Delivered," Planet Relish, November 1999

"More Memoirs of an Intergalactic Diplomat," A Winter Sampler, December 1998

"Playing Stick," Antipodean SF, February 1999; reprinted in Jackhammer, June 1999

"Cgxa 1001 - An Introduction to Comparative Galactic Xeno-Sociological Archeology," Jackhammer, November 1999

"Lest We Forget" published as **"The Memory of Death,"** Planet Relish, July 1999

"Bakemono," Parchment Symbols, October 1999

"Looking Into Paradox," SpaceWays Weekly, November 1999

"Peacemaker," Jackhammer, May 1999

"Peacekeeper," Jackhammer, June 1999

"Innocence," Exodus, February 1999

"Silence of the Croatan," Jackhammer, July 1998

"Fearful Symmetry," The Orphic Chronicle, May 1999

"Dance With Me, My Muse," 69 Flavors of Paranoia, May 1999

"Silence at the Ends of the Earth," Imelod, January 2000

ABOUT THE AUTHOR

Sean Campbell is a writer, software engineer and single father. Born in Ottawa Ontario, raised in Prince Edward Island, and currently living, working and raising his daughter in Calgary Alberta, has left Sean with a deep love and respect for the geographic and social diversity of Canada. When not writing fiction, or software code, Sean spends time building scale military models, and has several ship models on public display. He resides in a small townhouse with his daughter and an overweight guinea pig.

He also has a deep love and respect for grapefruit. Really. No kidding. Honest.

www.ingramcontent.com/pod-product-compliance
Lightning Source LLC
Chambersburg PA
CBHW050944050726
47592CB00007B/2420